A LIFE IN THE WILD

Volume One

A Life in the Wild
Volume One

Robin Stewart

NEW HAVEN PUBLISHING LTD UK

A Life in the Wild

First Edition
Published 2015
NEW HAVEN PUBLISHING LTD
www.newhavenpublishingltd.com
newhavenpublishing@gmail.com

Editor Val George
Cover photo © Lance Kirkly
Cover designs © Pete Cunliffe
pcunliffe@blueyonder.co.uk

newhaven
publishing

ISBN: 978-1-910705-13-1

Dedication

To Miss Poppy and her three brothers Zac, Fred and Jacob

Also by Robin Stewart

Being Mike Abbott

A Life in the Wild Volume 2
(Coming 2016)

A Letter From the Author

Dear Reader,

Without a past, there is no present; without a present, there can be no future. This story is a collection of many pasts and many presents, all leading to a future seen through the eyes of the animals that surround the old man in his present.

They are all controlled by Mother Nature. It is a journey seen through the eyes of many different souls, intertwined and held together by the same thread. Their connections are made, not because they are friends, but because they are part of the present—a life that surrounds an old man and his place and somehow connects them all. The destinies of each of the souls involved are controlled by the whims of Mother Nature and by how each soul is affected by her changes—not only by season but also by the effect the seasons have on the immediate environment and, of course, the intervention of every living things' foe: man himself.

The book is here to indulge your imagination whichever way you wish. So come in and enter the secret lives of animal and man as they live together and apart, joined together by Mother Nature and their love of life.

If you enjoy this book, feel free to send me a message on my website or Facebook page. I shall look forward to hearing from you.

Love and stuff

Robin

www.robin-stewart.com
https://www.facebook.com/FALCONNER?fref=ts

Table of Contents

ONE
It Started Here

The silence was shattered by a loud bang deep inside the old man's head and he awoke with a start to find himself clutching the arms of his leather chair. He put his right hand across his head and applied as much pressure as he could bear onto his left temple, with his left hand still grabbing the arm of the chair The old chair faced the large fire place that gave warmth and light to the old style kitchen and a place for wet dogs to dry as they stretched out in front of the hearth. Languishing in the heat, the dogs occasionally twitched when an ember spat onto their dreaming forms and interrupted whatever dogs feel in the warmth with their old mate for company.

From his vantage point in his comfy chair, he was near the Aga, the large combustion stove that always had a pot of coffee standing on it, sending out aromas that were hard to ignore. From here he also had a view of the sky through the window that looked out onto the veranda, where he often sat looking down on the day yards, the barns and the stables that housed his prized horses.

The pain in his head was slowly ebbing away; becoming a dull ache rather than a feeling like a red hot poker had been thrust into his brain. This was an intrusion that defied all pain barriers, entering with such force that there was no breath to take away; you were completely naked to the pain and to the fear.

It was not the first time this had happened and his doctor had said, 'Listen old man, it is something you just have to live with.' So he did; one day it might become a full-blown stroke, then again it might not, so until then it was just something that happened and you got over it.

Feeling much more in control and with the pain now a dull ache, he headed for one of his passions in life, the percolator that gave off the perfume that meant only one thing, coffee, a mixture of Columbian and Kenyan with a hint of blue, whatever that was. It was sent down to him by Tony, a mate who lived on the far side of Cairns in far north Queensland, who got it from a coffee specialist at the famous Cairns market.

Having poured his coffee and glanced out of the window at the yard below, he went back to his chair and reinstated himself, his thoughts drifting off to his foundation mare. She was a cross, her dam being a raw-boned New Zealand thoroughbred; big and rangy and fifteen three at the wither and her sire being a cross between a shire and a Percheron. The shire in her history added even more height and the Percheron gave a touch of the Arabian - and even more power.

So when he put his beloved Arabian stallions over her she produced foals that could lend themselves to many sports, from endurance to cross country, show jumping and dressage. Their versatility was unbeatable. It crossed his mind that he should really consult the birthing calendar as her time should be close; he put his coffee down on the side table and as always after one of these painful attacks, he seemed to doze off immediately, far away from the hurt that had intruded into his midday nap.

When he woke up in the late afternoon, the sky was leaden. A storm was brewing and the old man knew it was coming; he had seen all the signs and hoped that the mare had taken herself up to high ground.

When left to their own devices, for some unknown reason horses always seem to give birth just before or in the middle of the worst weather imaginable. Never on a balmy night with a full moon and the warmth of the day still lingering in the air; oh no, it had to be in or before a storm or a big freeze, as if to test the newborn's hardiness to make it or not. It almost sounded Shakespearian…

But he trusted the mare to know what the conditions would be, she had lived through many a birth and had always delivered and cared for her foal with the utmost motherly duty. He finished the last drop of coffee, managing with great confidence to stop just before the grounds that had escaped the filter could ruin the joy of a perfect cup of coffee.

He made his way down from the veranda and collected three bails of straw from the barn before entering the stable and scattering the straw evenly over the floor. If by any chance he needed to bring the mare and foal back to the farm, there would be a warm and comforting stable ready and waiting. He then repeated the exercise in the other stable, just in case he needed to bring the stallion down as well.

His semi-retired competition stallion was way up the hill in his own domain - a well fenced ten acre paddock with a stream running along its northern boundary and well placed trees for shelter and to give shade from the relentless Australian sun. It was a life of comparative luxury for his friend and faithful campaigner of many an endurance ride, his genes had been passed on to many of the foals that the old man had bred over the years and they had never failed him, he seemed to give his offspring all of his good points and none of his annoying little foibles that every horse has.

By the time he had finished and closed the second stable door, the rumbling had already started and small drops of rain were starting to fall. The old man knew there was much worse to come and made his way back to the homestead before the droplets turned into large unforgiving globules of hard stinging rain made even more vengeful as the wind picked up and the clouds suddenly became jet black.

He had just closed the kitchen door when the first bolt of lightning struck and the thunder clap was more than just deafening, it was all-encompassing and crashed around him making the house tremble and shake. This was going to be a real buster, and as he stoked up the fire and placed emergency candles within reach of his chair, he gave a thought to the big mare high up on the hill and hoped that all was well and that she was safe. He sat down in his chair with a glass of red wine in one hand and the full coffee mug on the table beside him. The fire sprang to life and the dogs stretched out feeling secure in the heat and they waited for the thunder and lightning to do its worst.

The next day was overcast and cool; it had been one of those strange mornings where after feeding up and doing all the necessary bits and pieces, he found himself sitting in the tack room, the dogs sprawled out in front of the unlit slow combustion stove. The old man was looking around at all the bits and pieces in the tack room, the heavy harness left over from the days when he would put one of his horses between the shafts and drive his buggy or cart out and about just for fun, allowing his thoughts to wander aimlessly as they ambled along, when he suddenly noticed the end of a piece of timber with a strange sort of drawing on it. He reached up and pulled the plank out of its tightly fitting hiding place to reveal the name plate that an artist friend of his had made years ago. At one end was the figure of a slightly portly toad dressed for battle with a sword and a musket thrust into his belt like a musketeer, and at the other end was the same toad lying down with his portly tummy facing skyward, with the words 'poop poop' in a small balloon above his head. It was obviously the toad from *The Wind in the Willows,* one of the old man's favourite stories, and toad was his all-time hero, because he was an adventurer and a dreamer who achieved everything and nothing without really hurting anyone but himself. And low and behold, between the two images of the famous and magnificent Toad were these beautifully inscribed words: *TOAD'S ABODE.*

Why on earth he had never put it on the gate - maybe because he thought that someone would steal it - he could not remember, so he immediately dusted it off and wandered off to the barn to look for some of that Swedish weather-proof oil that he knew was lurking in there somewhere. Once he had given his new-found treasure a coat of weather proofing, then he would decide where to hang it, for this farmstead surely was *TOAD'S ABODE* and the sign should be up somewhere where he and his entourage of horses, dogs, peacocks and chickens - not forgetting the bookends, his two cats, and Ollie his beloved owl, lived in a particular kind of harmony in this troubled world.

So the old man strode off on a mission of the utmost importance - the completion of his sanctuary - the name plate that said it all: *TOAD'S ABODE.*

TWO
New Life

It was late in the afternoon, and the early chill had a feel to it, a warning of worse to come. The sky had turned a pale sea green with a hint of ice blue at the edges and the old grey mare knew her time had come. The life that she had carried through the hot serene days of summer was due on what was to become one of the coldest nights of the late winter.

Skirting past the fairy wood, the mare had doggedly climbed to the top of the hill paddock, stopping many times to breath deep and long; each rest period coming sooner than the last. Until with her head low to the ground, nostrils flaring and sides heaving, she finally reached her goal. The storm had passed over on her journey and she could face the next stage without the relentless rain.

There was no fear in the mare; she had foaled many times before and knew the signs well. The little tweaks at her sides, the fluttering on her flanks, made her swing round and nip at the air, missing the ungainly mound that sat between fore and back legs. Her only concern now was to try to find shelter for the foal that she would undoubtedly have by morning.

The mare surveyed her domain. Behind her the valley floor, long and winding; the paddocks defined only by the tree lines along the river bank, or the occasional glint from a piece of new barbed wire joining rusty bits of fence together.

She hoped she had managed to climb above the frost line. Not that it wasn't still cold; the eerie feeling that surrounded her meant only one thing; tomorrow would bring a harsh white covering that would burn the new shoots and numb the feet.

He was definitely due. She seemed to know she was carrying a colt, a busy colt, who was bored with darkness and was starting his journey into the unknown. The mare slowly sank to the ground and the birth began to take its course.

When the colt emerged, the mare licked him clean. Methodically and very tenderly she had torn the life-protecting sack from his muzzle and allowed the air to penetrate his nostrils. The shock of his first breath had brought a tremor with it that made him shudder uncontrollably. As his lungs filled a second time, he experienced an overwhelming feeling of well-being… life was coursing through his veins. He nickered and gave himself a shock at the strange noise. The mare breathed on him, making a snuffling sound as her nostrils fluttered over his neck and the colt felt safe, and rested his head on his outstretched front legs.

It was a long time before he managed to stand up and keep himself steady enough to take his first drink. The mares' udder was full and the steady drips of colostrum, thickly sweet and full of goodness, beckoned until he was firmly latched onto her teat sucking frantically, his tail swishing from side to side.

Later, the colt awoke with a shock. It seemed as if his muzzle had grown wings and was desperately trying to take off. He pulled his head back as if to dislodge his new appendage. His eyes rolled back and he started an involuntary stretch. As he shakily stood and nuzzled the mare, the wings on the end of his nose were forgotten. The butterfly, for that is what it was, turned its attention to a clump of fireweed and continued to dance in the early morning sun.

Up in the high paddock the mare kept the colt away from any outside influence that could confuse or upset him. She enjoyed being alone with her foals for as long as possible. All too soon the inquisitive nature of her offspring led to interrupted grazing and irritability, which was not conducive to the mother-son relationship needed to promote a foal's education.

They stayed at the top end of the hill paddock for the next two weeks. By now the colt had been accustomed to the sight of the two ginger cats coming out of the tree line, heading for the long since deserted old school house. He was fascinated at the way they would bush up their tails and run hither and thither, somersaulting over each other and then, with ears flattened tight to their heads, pull themselves upright and hurl into mock battle, only to separate and lie down, eyes closed and tail-tips twitching.

The colt would then raise his tail and prance off stiff-legged, looking left and right, then stop and open his nostrils wide and blow out noisily, only to realise that he had moved further from his mother than he wanted to, then race back and find comfort at her side. Yes, life was pure joy on top of the hill and he was at peace with the world.

The fine weather broke early one evening; the atmosphere changed with a rustling in the evergreens, gusts of wind that caused the younger gums to bend and lean in unison. Black cockatoos had spent the last few hours screeching their storm warning and sea birds had started to fly inland looking for a safe refuge. Then the storm broke with a fury that only the mother of all nature could explain.

The mare kept her back to the wind, moving her hind legs sideways so that the rain always hit her rump, for driving rain straight onto the face was one of the most unpleasant things that a horse could imagine. The colt was charging back and forth, kicking and snorting and challenging the storm. That was until the first clap of thunder. He thought the ground would burst and swallow him up. The flash of lightning that preceded it had pulled him up short and he screamed as the bright light shot in a diagonal jagged line, dancing and flashing as it earthed itself into the ground. He was shaking almost uncontrollably. The rolling thunder crashed around him and he experienced a feeling of fear, of ever-diminishing size, as if he were shrinking.

The old mare stood very still; the colt ran to her, not managing to stop in time, colliding hard with her flank. She nickered, he reared, she nickered again and he stood, rigid, not daring to move. She blew out, her nostrils fluttering, the warm breath caressing his muzzle, transmitting calmness and a feeling of great strength.

The massive trees on the edge of the hill paddock, the really big mighty gums that stood so strong and tall, gave branches up to the storm, dropping them with a mighty crashing sound, splintering into a thousand fragments on landing. The wind howled and the rain drove into the ground, stinging them on the way down, and they stood side by side, joined together by an invisible thread, a bond deeper than reason itself. The mare's logic was being passed on to her offspring: if you can't run from it and you can't fight it, stay still and eventually it will leave.

And as the storm raged around them, the colt felt safe and somehow he knew he would never be scared again. He stamped one foot and nudged his mothers' neck. She put her head on his shoulder and blew gently and the colt closed his eyes and slept out the storm, as only a horse can.

The storm had long since passed when the old mare took the colt down to the fairy wood. The rushing water fascinated him. The rivers had risen and the waterways were self-cleansing. Along with the old fence posts and logs that had come down in the flood, there were strange looking creatures with claws and nippers, hard backed and beady-eyed. The freshwater crayfish had been swept downstream and were now looking for safety in the big pools of water that had collected. There were other horses on the opposite bank, but they could not cross the swollen torrent of water. So the colt and his mother had the fairy wood to themselves.

There were pathways through the wood, well worn by cattle and horse. The young colt took to galloping along these tracks at a great speed, tossing his head and kicking up his heels. The old mare ignored his play as she had seen it all before. She always brought her offspring down to the wood so that they might learn the art of twisting and turning at full gallop, ducking the low branches so as to miss the broad, mitten-shaped leaves of the stinging tree, that seemed to serve no other purpose than to sting and then itch for hours, making the skin twitch uncontrollably.

The young colt had been standing under the outstretched branches of one of the big privet trees that lined the river bank, when the curlews' alarm call started. He hadn't paid that much attention to their incessant screeching as they always screamed first and looked later, so that any creature that might need advance warning could high-tail it - only to look back after a considerable distance and when a safe vantage point had been reached.

On this particular day he found himself looking across the river, fixing his gaze to the flats beyond, to see if he could spot the reason for the curlew's agitation. …Nothing, absolutely nothing. He could see one of the ginger cats lying on a tree stump and there was the big red dog, who never seemed to go anywhere without the man in the tweed coat, sleeping soundly on the school house steps.

The curlews suddenly screeched with a different kind of urgency; the colt's head came up quickly. The birds were on the move and their tone had an edge to it, an agitation, a warning. The water sprayed out and upwards as the colt leaped forwards through the river. He had to know, he had to find out what had caused the birds to change their call.

The birds were on the far side of the flats and the colt increased his pace even more, throwing his front legs up high and outwards. He came to a sudden halt and stiffened; it was there, it was different and all of a sudden he was completely on guard. It was a new sensation, not fear, only alertness, awareness, of what?

The curlews had stopped their cries, the cat was still curled up on the stump and the red dog was now sitting up and absentmindedly looking out across the flats and onto the ridge above.

Just below the timber line there was a flicker, a brief movement… the red dog lifted her nose, breathed in, savoured the smells that were wafting on the slight breeze and came up with nothing. She stretched, yawned and lay down to once again enjoy the late afternoon sun.

The colt snorted once more then relaxed, swished his tail and slowly headed back. The puzzle could not be solved tonight. And as the sun started to streak into the light puffy clouds of the evening sky, the colt and his mother moved to slightly higher ground. It would be a clear night with a big, bright, very cold and unforgiving moon.

THREE
The Pack

High up on the hill a tawny owl turned his head one hundred and sixty degrees to follow the footfalls of the six dogs as they moved steadily through the bush, hardly visible, tongues lolling to one side, silent pads hitting the dirt with uniform regularity. For those that knew of them, the pack had returned.

It was mid-afternoon when the lead bitch had reached the valley floor, leaving the other five dogs a quarter of the way up on the edge of the national park, just waiting. Each dog acted on the unspoken word; survival had taught them well and being of mixed domestic and wild blood, their fear of man was non-existent, but their knowledge of him was vast.

No sooner had the bitch found a good vantage point from which she could assess the old school house and its resident foes, than the curlews had spotted her. The only way to deal with curlews is to ignore them and flatten into the ground; if you do not recognise their existence then they tend after a short while, to ignore yours.

The bitch had seen the red dog sniff the air; she was downwind and up high with no chance of her scent lingering. She had turned her attention to the young colt, watching with vague amusement as he pranced about. This was how it always was with young horses, all bluff and no follow up. Then having finished her investigations she faded back into the forest; the pack followed her lead and adopted her loping gait as she padded along the once well-worn trail.

The bitch ran with her nose down, glued to the recently laid scent of a foraging wallaby, her eyes looking straight ahead so that if the wallaby came into sight she would transfer to vision and increase her speed to the kill. They followed the trail to the edge of a rock wall and down a track carved tight against imposing ledges. These narrow and sometimes perilous laneways had become established over years of small feet carving out a route and then rains coursing through and eventually turning them into narrow highways from the top ledges to the valleys below. They very soon dropped down to a well-hidden wide flat ledge, littered with odd pieces of shale and rocks.

Having lost the scent of the wallaby, the bitch had stopped; she and the pack lingered to drink and then they re-marked their territory - it had been nine months since the last time they were here and they were advertising that they were back. The local dingos and any feral dogs that might be around would very soon be aware of their presence, usually to their misfortune. This pack was a tightly formed group and they hunted, slept, played and ran as one.

They could hear the newborn calves calling to their mothers on the valley floor below, and one by one they started to pick where to sprawl and wait for dusk to overtake the valley. If luck was with them, they would feed well tonight.

The colt stood mid-stream, the water swirling around the bottom of his tendons and it made them feel tight and springy. There was still that cold edge to the water that made tingles run up and down his legs; a good and exciting feeling, yet something was missing, something was not quite right, something… he leapt upward and outward, clearing the bank, acting in the grip of panic. His head came up as soon as his foreleg touched the ground and he gave a high, shrill scream; he felt lost and desolate. From the fairy wood came a nicker, a reassuring sound and he knew that he was safe, there was his safety blanket: the old grey mare, the source of warm milk and comfort. He was so overtaken at this feeling of loss and panic that he ran straight into her flank, spinning and kicking out behind. The mare put her ears back and snapped half-heartedly at his rump.

Then the colt fell in behind her as she wound her way through the fairy wood and slowly up the hill. There was no real urgency to her stride yet there was great purpose, a feeling as old as time itself; to know you should not be where you are, that you should move on somewhere else - just go, no rush, just leave. It is a sense handed down by Mother Nature and not to be disregarded.

The days became hot and sometimes very humid. The bitch and her pack had ranged far and wide, using the wide ledge as their base camp. That first night that they went down to the valley below they had tried to bring down a young calf, only to feel the sharp horns of the Brahman cross cow that was its mother. The dogs had backed off and travelled to the next valley to hunt, more than one of them limping from the cloven-hoofed attack.

Farm buildings did not make them feel nervous or trapped as a true dingo would. They were recognised instead as places to find an easy meal…

At the old man's farm a stray chicken had eluded the night time gathering to the chook shed and had fluffed up over a clutch of eggs that she had laid in a half open tool box in the barn.

She was oblivious to the dogs' stealthy entry. The hen knew nothing, from nest to jaws, the bitch had taken less than thirty seconds to scent her. The eggs were quickly cracked and swallowed by expert jaws.

In the stallion's stable, nostrils flared and ears pricked forward. Deep in his subconscious was an area that never slept, always alert, ready to react instantly. From a scent in the air a memory had been aroused of a cold, stark night; one of his mares was down in the river, muscles cramping in her attempts to foal. Her efforts to eject the colt had been exhausting, she had felt herself slide into the water; then there were the dogs, surrounding and attacking. The bitch's scent had never left him; she was an enemy with no apparent fear, snapping at the mare's nose then rushing around and pulling on the now dead foal. His attempts to arrest the attack were futile and now here it was again, that same scent right here in his domain.

He screamed his warning into the night and then it was gone and he could no longer pick up the smell that had jogged his memory so vividly. He snorted once more and then turned his back on the night.

The bitch was trotting out, followed by the rest of the pack, making her way back up the hill that would return them to the ridge above. From there she could look down on both the valleys and assess the hunting strategy for the remainder of the night.

FOUR
Change

From his vantage point the colt could see the commotion on the flats and it made no sense at all. There were lots of people and lots of horses and things that horses came out of. It was just too much for the colt, his curiosity was bursting and nothing would stop him now. As he got closer to the river he paused then advanced again till he was standing on the bank, looking across at the strange but fascinating scenario on the opposite bank. There were horses standing in squares made of white floating stuff that just seemed to hang in the air, and horses walking to and fro and not really going anywhere at all…

What he was witnessing was a gathering for the sport of endurance riding - an incredibly popular sport in Australia. The competitors came for the amazing terrain and Arab buyers came each year to choose horses to take back to the United Arab Emirates or Saudi Arabia. Bloodlines in Australia were being bred with this sport in mind: tough, hardy Arabians that could withstand hot, cold and harsh conditions, as the sport encompassed all of Australia, from the cold of Tasmania to the heat of the tropics. When in hard competition these horses would travel at incredible speeds and to complete an 80km ride in four hours was common for owners at the top end of the competitive market looking to sell their horses on for large amounts of money.

The purists in the gathering were very happy just to enjoy the scenery and finish the ride within the time allotted, as the motto for endurance was 'to complete is to win'. This did not always apply to the gung-ho 'rip shit and bust' fraternity who would ride like the devil possessed only to 'vet out' after 40km, often endangering their horses and taking home a very lame horse, or even worse a horse with a bad metabolic condition which can cause awful internal injuries.

The greed factor in any form of winning to make a profit can, to the inexperienced, have terrible consequences - especially for the horse that is too fat or too thin, under trained, overtrained - the list goes on and on.

The colt snorted, stamped, snorted again, and as he was looking straight ahead he did not see the man leaning against a tree just to the left of centre, the red bitch motionless at his side, the only movement a slight roll of the thumb over the forefinger as a cigarette took shape in his hands.

He had stood like this often, watching, as the young colt became more and more familiar with the world around him. The red bitch was used to this procedure as she had done this many times before, lying at his feet, while the man in the tweed coat stood and watched. Each season for as long as she could remember, this had been the way of it. There was a tiny crack as the match ignited and a thin line of smoke headed upwards. The colt spun round and fixed his stare on the blue smoke streamer as it got caught on the breeze. The man turned and walked away, leaving the colt standing alone. In total disgust he snorted, shook his head, half reared, sat back on his haunches, leapt up, spun round and took off at an incredible speed back towards the serenity that surrounded the old mare. One thing was for sure; unknowingly the young colt was soon to experience a new chapter in his so far carefree life.

People nodded as the man walked slowly down the line of electric fences, the red bitch at his side. There was a blur of black, blue and white and a second dog was at his heels. The German coolie cross pinned back her ears and grinned, the brown eye soft and gentle, the wall-eye, blue and unfeeling. And so, blue eye facing out, she walked beside her friend, the three of them in perfect harmony. It would have taken a very insensitive type to interrupt their commune together as the strength and pride between them was palpable.

The air had a slight crispness to it as the old man slowly climbed up through the hill paddock, a loose rope in his hand, the end of which was attached to a light braid halter. The tall Arab stallion matched his pace, neither were blowing hard, neither were straining. They had both done this journey together many times and the stallion always matched his friend's pace. Whatever the speed the man set, the stallion was with him, never pulling, never straining against him, always right there with him, joined by an invisible cord - a respect well-earned and bonded strongly over the years. The stallion knew that when the man's head came up and his shoulders straightened, that within two strides he would stop and turn, always looking back down to the valley below, never up, as if not to be daunted by the continuous climb. And somehow seeming to get strength from his achievement so far, there they would stand, the wildness in both of them controlled, yet all-encompassing. The stallion snorted and they turned in tandem and continued their journey up the hill.

Lying on the flat rock collecting the first warm rays of the day, the bitch had watched them climbing closer and closer for the last hour as they had slowly wended their way upward. It was of no great concern to her, as she could slip quietly away at any given point and not leave a trace. Also, the man did not carry the stick that made a noise before knocking a dog sideways never to get up and run again. And without it, man was slow and clumsy and of no real threat to such a free spirit as herself.

On reaching the crest, the man stopped and his two faithful dogs, who never missed an opportunity to travel with their friend, lay down. He slipped off the halter and the stallion shook his head and blew out noisily.

The bitch registered simply that here was a man, two dogs and a horse; two male, two female, the rest was irrelevant. Her priority, which was simple, was her matriarchy in regards to the pack, her survival, and then her unborn pups. Soon that order would change, with birth becoming more and more imminent, the order of priority would be different. Her pups first, then her survival, and the pack could always be controlled. Lifting up her head she combined yawning and stretching in the same movement and then laid her head back down onto her outstretched paws. Life was running its course.

The young colt was confused; since he had become aware of the old man he had registered the man and the two dogs many times but always from a safe distance. They didn't worry him unduly, as they never made a move towards him. Yet today was different in some way. He had been grazing away from his mother when he suddenly became aware that she had walked towards the old man, her head stretched out, nickering softly. The man was standing directly in front of her, a rope and halter in his hand. He pulled something red out of his pocket and held it out for the mare to sniff and then she gently took it out of his hand with the softest of lips. The man then slipped the halter over her head and they set off down the slope together, the dogs tucking in behind.

The colt whinnied and arched his neck, tossed his head and broke straight into a canter, galloping past the two dogs and the man who seemed to be attached to his mother by a long piece of something the likes of which he had not seen before. By this time he had started kicking his heels high in the air.

The man ignored him completely, as did the mare and the red dog. The only recognition he got was from the wall-eyed bitch, who lifted a lip as he sailed past. She would never do any more than that. It was just a warning: don't come too close too fast.

It was no surprise to the old man to see the colt, after rushing past and away at such speed, come striding back towards them, if striding is the right word. For this would have to have been the most exaggerated, fully extended prance imaginable. Head and neck arched to a degree that might ordinarily be created only by a false aid like a Market Harborough, commonly known by some as a German bridle or Martingale, and consequently called over bent.

By the time the procession had reached the bottom gate it looked for all intents and purposes like a family outing: man, dogs and horse in a parallel line with the colt's head safely tucked in behind his mother's rump.

The man closed the gate and headed for the yards at the back of the farm house, this was what people called his top farm; the old school house was a sort of folly that doubled up as a place where friends could stay when they came to visit. Over the years he had come to the conclusion that the way to mix and match people, however close they might be, was to keep them at a distance. He would reside between them and socialise as the urge took him. He no longer had deadlines to meet or people to answer to, just his dogs and his horses and a collection of dreams.

He had relinquished the stress of a public image and had slipped into the tranquillity of simplicity, Mother Nature's way of giving the soul a place to rest and find solace; sounds easy, yet no mean feat in the crowded stress-ridden world that man has created in the name of progress. The company he kept had no idea as to his history; to them he was the old man they had come to love and trust; who had he once been? It really didn't matter.

The colt followed his mother into the large stable and as she turned round and out again he found himself enclosed on all sides by the restricting walls. The man had closed both the bottom and the top of the stable door and there was no view or way out. He screamed loudly and heard the gentle nicker of his mother's answer and quieted to reassess his surroundings. The smells that shared his new home were strange, yet not fearful; there was an overwhelming scent, a pungent, strong aroma that suggested a power that he had never encountered before: a strength that somehow made him feel secure if not a little confused.

The young colt had no idea that this was the stallion's stable, the stallion being his sire; in horse terminology, the royal term of sire is used instead of father.

Outside the afternoon shadows were beginning to slowly creep across the landscape and evening was approaching, cows were slowly returning to their night time pastures after milking, and the school bus had long since dropped off its charges and a gentle stillness overtook the rolling hills that surrounded the picturesque farm that now had a new arrival firmly ensconced within the safety of its confines.

FIVE
A Raid

High up upon the hill the dog pack was getting ready to forage for their evening meal. The bitch rose, shook herself, and sat back down again. She bit at her flank and snarled at a younger dog who had come over to touch noses; she would not be hunting tonight. Her time had almost come and as the pack made its move down the hill she waited and then started to climb up to a safe ledge that adjoined a cave that she had picked out earlier as the right and safest place to have her pups.

An old wily dog was leading the pack, with a younger female nearly abreast as they loped out of the timber line and down towards the valley floor. As the lead bitch had gone looking for privacy, it was up to the most pushy and possibly foolhardy of the remaining bitches to vie for the position at the head of the pack, for to run up front needs a little more wisdom than just a snarl and snapping teeth. The lead dog is responsible for the whole pack, for where you lead, they will follow. It is important for the pack's survival that those up front have a good knowledge of tactics, alert noses and most importantly, the ability to resist foolhardy temptation, and to develop the age old art of calculating patience.

At the very back of the cave, where the light was dim and the roof was low, the bitch was nursing the two remaining bundles of still slightly damp fur. She had given birth to six perfectly formed puppies, four of which had been stillborn. The two remaining pups were not small and having no competition for the teat would obviously grow fast. Their stomachs now full, and with eyes tightly closed, the pups were contented and knew nothing of their changed environment from womb to cave.

The bitch cast her gaze across her small litter of two, and around the sides of the cave. Secure in herself that all was well, she spun on one hind leg and was across the ledge and over the side. She hurled herself to the right and onto a small craggy track; it was only a hundred or so metres further on that she stopped and lapped greedily from a small pool of brackish water. Having quenched her thirst she sprang back up the hill and in under a minute was back in the cave, her tiny pups hardly stirred as she curled around them and stretched, closed her eyes, and slept.

The colt woke with a start; he had eventually settled into his new surroundings because he knew that the mare was close and, as he could not see out of the stable, it was comparatively simple for him to switch off. And even though he would every now and then visibly tremble, he waited in limbo. He had heard the mare next door which was of comfort to him but it did not enlighten him at all as to what was happening outside.

The colt could hear the frantic panting as the dog pack padded past. And a barking from a distance, then there was a thump and then a high pitched sound, once again a thump, and then silence.

The red dog and Squint growling in unison had awoken the old man, who had dozed off in the comfort of his armchair. The feral pack, with a young bitch, being impetuous and inexperienced, had pushed the lead dog very quickly along the valley floor and straight to the old man's farm. Her memory of easy pickings from the barn had clouded any sense of caution. Paying little attention to the direction of the wind or the dim light in the farmhouse, she had ignored the barn and had gone straight to the chicken coup, going round and round looking for an entry point. She got hold of the wire netting where it joined the corner pole and arching her back like a bow had dug all four feet into the ground and propelled herself backwards. She managed to dislodge an old staple and stretched the wire, which afforded her a small opening. She was through in a flash, throwing caution to the wind and grabbing at the very first bundle of feathers she came across.

The noise that a chicken makes when it is rudely interrupted from its sleep and tugged out of the nest by its tail feathers has crescendos not easily imaginable by those who have never experienced it.

The fat Rhode Island Red hen had the cruellest of awakenings. It was just as the hen, flapping her wings uncontrollably, had somehow extricated herself from the young bitch's hold that the old man fired, catching her just as she had leapt up to re-grab the escaping chicken, the sound of her frustration dying in her throat. As she crumpled onto the floor the rest of the pack seemed to just fade away, merging into night shadows. Twenty or more hens joined their hysterical companion in her incessant clamour. The old man fired one more shot vertically, more out of annoyance than anything else, placed the rifle on the veranda table and flipped the outside switch, flooding the yard with light.

The colt heard the old man walking across the yard, pulling and opening the chook shed door. And through the tiniest of cracks in the slab wall of the stable he watched as the old man turned the now inactive intruder over and then, much to his annoyance had then moved out of his field of vision.

The old man had studied the inert form for the time that it took to ascertain age, sex, condition of coat, teeth, and off course, present state of health, which was not too time consuming under the circumstances.

Having finished his scrutiny of the situation he walked back to the house and climbed the four wooden steps to the veranda, turned right, stopped and leant on the guard rail looking out across the floodlit yard and into the shadows beyond.

In the ash tray next to the chair a thin plume of smoke rose from one of the few indulgences he allowed himself from times past, a Romeo No 2, a smaller version of the large Romeo and Julieta that he used to smoke. He had found that nowadays he would manage to enjoy seventy five percent of the cigar before he put it into the ashtray and he succumbed to the solace of his favourite chair. He sighed, breathed in deeply through his nose and out through pursed lips, turned towards the light switch and with one flick the yard returned to darkness. The colt once again shifted his weight and returned to a state of calm, the horse limbo that usually ends up with a lowered head and deep, uninterrupted breathing.

Picking up his cigar the man mused on the dog in the chicken coup. Was she part of the ever-returning feral pack? It seemed unlikely, the matriarch was too experienced a hunter to allow one of her underlings to charge into a chook pen. Maybe she was out of the picture and had met with what could be classed as a 'just fate', even though the initial problem of her release into the bush started with man. Once survival without a benefactor took over, unfortunately for her, she had become a public enemy.

He rose quickly, stubbing the remainder of the cigar into the ashtray. What if she was close to dropping a litter of pups? It would be most unsatisfactory to have her whelp here. It would mean she would stay in the area till her offspring were old enough to travel - not a good scenario at all.

His forefinger wrapped around the neck of the standard lamp, he felt for the switch and as his thumb pushed firmly inwards the farmhouse became as one with the night.

Out in his paddock, the stallion had heard the panting and the sound of twigs breaking and knew that his domain was about to be invaded. He snorted, arched his neck, blew hard and long, making the veins that lay beneath his skin stand out like the River Nile in flood. Vision was minimal so the stallion started going from side to side, only a few paces in each direction at first, lengthening his stride as he sorted the air, inhaling and exhaling, picking up speed, his head held ridiculously high, making him look like a Centaur. With nostrils flared, teeth flashing and hooves beating down, making the earth vibrate with his power - the sound alone put fear into the hearts of the staunchest adversary.

The fleeing dogs thought that they were out of the reach of trouble and as they were in need of a rest after their arduous climb did not expect to be confronted by this formidable creature.

The dog that had been pushed so hard by the young bitch on the way out was the first to breast the hill. The sheer adrenalin rush that this vision caused the over tired dog made him leap diagonally away. The moment he hit the ground his exhaustion showed. The stallion, quick to see the advantage, attacked with a curdling scream that pierced the night. With teeth bared, nostrils flared and ears flat to his scull he threw himself forward and pounded the ground at all angles.

As the dog ducked down he had thrown his hindquarters backwards. Consequently the hoof that was meant for his head missed, connecting instead with his outstretched front leg taking three of his toes clean off. The dog, screaming with the shock of this new and unbelievably sharp pain had slid backward another foot or so only to discover that there was no more bank and his exit from the already one-sided battle was none too elegant.

He rolled over two, three, four times, his throbbing paw seeming to come into constant contact with something hard, sending shockwaves up his leg. His descent now meant he had the climb once again in front of him. With the joint pains of foot and now bruised ribs, it would be a slow and arduous journey.

As the rest of the dog pack came over the ridge, they were instantly aware that all was not as it should be. The pack split into four, each travelling at a different angle, yet all heading for the beginning of the next dense timberline. This encounter was a rare 'in your face' experience, more terrifying than their encounters with man, and they pulled on every reserve to reach the trees unseen. Once there, they faded silently away, leaving the old wounded dog to look out for himself.

The following morning found the old man making the long and arduous climb back up the hill to the stallion's paddock. He had disposed of last night's interloper by piling logs around the inert form and then dosing it liberally with diesel; set it on fire, leaving only a small burnt patch on the ground.

He followed the dogs' trail until it became clear that the only place they could be going was the high ridge that linked the many plateaus of the range together. Head down, leaning into the slope, he continued upward. He knew as soon as he saw the stallion that they had passed this way. His fine and usually glossy coat was smeared with the remains of dried sweat, leaving white wavy lines of salt across his back. The old man could only guess what had transpired and after going over his friend with meticulous hands was pleased to find that he only looked the worse for wear. So gently slipping on the lightly braided rope halter that always lived around his waist for just such changes in plan, he started the long walk back down to the valley. The stallion would be spending some more time back at the farm, at least until he had a better idea of what the dog pack was doing.

The frogmouth owl is a territorial bird and Oliver was no different from his counterparts. He had been raised at the farm and had begun his life enjoying the delights of fine top grade mince, not exactly the diet that the wildlife carers would have suggested he be fed had they been informed of his rescue. From a very young and incredibly vulnerable age he was under the umbrella of an upbringing that could only be described as multi-cultural.

As he grew older he would fly in and out of the farmhouse whenever he pleased, sitting wherever he felt like, paying no mind to the two red cats and the resident dogs. Usually he was puffed up like a furry marshmallow, but every now and then he would assume the 'I am a stick, look somewhere else' manner. This very thin and puny act could be induced by the old man mimicking the noise of the wings of an eagle or similar bird of prey beating down upon him; a noise that the man would make by sucking air in through pursed lips and out again. Their shared pantomime always made the old man chuckle and if Ollie was perched on a low enough protrusion, the old man would scratch him under his outstretched chin. Within thirty seconds or so Ollie would shake his feathers, lift his tail and, and once relieved, would resume the puffed up marshmallow pose once again. It was Ollie, from a tree on the fringes of the high plateau, who bore witness to a turning point in the feral dog pack's hierarchy.

It was long past dawn as the injured dog finally climbed the last stretch leading up to the safety of the high plateau. The pain in his side had lost none of its intensity; only his sheer doggedness had kept him heading upward.

He had just begun to level out when for no reason other than instinct, something made him turn in his tracks. The large hound hit him fair and square on his injured side, extracting a loud yet mournful sound as his adversary sank his teeth into his now totally exposed neck. His exit from this world was quick and expedient.

The large hound was an expert at his trade, trained to bowl a wild pig over and then sink his large canines deep into the jugular, leaning back and tearing out the throat. He had been out alone in the bush for three weeks, living only with excruciating pain, then thirst and a nagging hunger. He had been caught off guard by a large boar some weeks back and still carried the angry red scars left by the enraged pig's tusks.

The hound rose and walked slowly over to the stiffening remains of the old dog and rolled unceremoniously all over it; a sure-fire way of showing his contempt for the late adversary and serving to cover his own pungent scent.

He shook his big, shaggy head and loped off up the hill. His breeding was a hotchpotch of Mastiff, Deerhound, Irish Wolfhound and Bull Terrier. The crisscrossing of the hound and bull had for years been the breeding stock of the celebrated pigging dog, a loyal and faithful dog to his human family, yet having all the attributes of a true killing machine.

Although he had not yet met up with the feral pack, he was to play a key part in its future.

SIX
Lessons Begin

Before leaving to check on the stallion, the old man had opened the top door to the colt's stable and the colt watched with interest as the man and his proud companion had walked back into the yard area. The old man hitched the stallion up to a peg on the wall and proceeded to turn on the tap at the side of the shed. Releasing a jet of water from the loosely hanging hose, the stallion snorted as the stream of water hit his flank. The wavy lines of sweat and congealed dust slowly dissolved and poured off him.

When the old man had finished and the stallion was shining, he went back to the tap, drinking from the hose as he turned off the water supply. He reached up and took down the half-moon shaped scraper that would take off any excess water and allow him to feel any scabs or hidden abrasions. He did not expect to find anything wrong yet he always checked, even when the stallion had only been in his house paddock for the day.

The old man had scraped the stallion almost dry, his fingers going over tendon and back with methodical expertise, not a skerrick of an area was left untouched and only when he was totally satisfied that all was well did he stop his search, relinquishing the scraper and starting to brush the glistening coat with long, kind yet firm strokes.

As the brush travelled down the stallion's neck he stretched out his head and curled his lip, pointing his nose sideways as only a horse can do. He seemed to find a great contentment in the man's attentions. Occasionally he would snap his teeth together, swinging his head and grimacing, especially when the brush touched a really ticklish spot. Even without the loosely tied halter rope the stallion would never do more than stamp and twitch, shaking his head and snapping his teeth. The horse loved the feeling of release that came after each stamp and shake, the man, by following the brush stroke with inquisitive fingers, sorting through those tiny tight little sinews which, when aided by the horse's reaction to his fingers, released their hold.

Both parties had long ago agreed that this grooming exercise was of mutual benefit to them, most importantly, it was the continuation of the bond between them, both having their own forms of expertise as leaders, yet never competing, always acknowledging that they never intruded into personal space, an area that was mutually agreed upon by both parties. Sounds complicated, but it is simply called respect.

The old man laid his hand flat on the Arab's rump, the stallion danced as if giving a brief encore, then he stood rock still, like a noble statue, then shook as if his life depended on it, concluding with an enormous exclamation through his nostrils. He snorted once more, finishing off with a shake of his head combined with a couple of half-hearted phfff's, turned to face the man, dropped his head and waited for the halter to be removed.

The old man unhooked the halter rope and walked across the yard to the tack room, closely followed by 'Himself'. This was the name that he always referred to the stallion. His fashionable stage name was for those who liked to make comment on a horse's bloodlines. He just figured; he's Himself.

He placed the bridle over an old boat anchor suspended from a long round pole by an old heavy chain that hung just inside the door. It was the 'hang it here first' hook, to be moved at a later date to wherever it lived in the first place. He turned in the doorway. 'Might as well start on the colt,' he thought, 'I'll be keeping Himself at home till I know what's happening with those damn dogs.'

He stroked the stallion under his chin, watching with a smile as Himself started to extend his neck to a ridiculous length.

"You're a hopeless case," he said. "Tomorrow it's back to basics. I'd better tell Trevor to come and trim the big mare and you, and then come back in a week and trim the colt and shoe you both. I think we should give the mare a rest this season and throw her out just to graze and get fat - give her a rest from foals for a year or two."

Not since his back had been operated on had he shod a horse and before then he would always consult with TB on anything that was different to the norm. TB's first comment every time the old man phoned him was,

"Oh jeez, mate, I try to keep away from those big bastards, you know that."

Today was no exception.

"Yes, well, doesn't lean you reckon? Mate she leans and I'm out of there. I mean I am gone. I do not and I mean categorically I do not need nearly a ton of big mare sitting on my old frame. Alright?"

The old man put the phone down, poured a cup of thick black coffee into a very small cup, added two heaped teaspoons of brown sugar and slowly wandered out onto the veranda. There was nothing like the veranda when some thinking was the order of the day.

Trevor had arrived to do his day's work at the farm and was working on the colt.

"Not going too bad. I shouldn't say that, he'll probably kick me now." A small chuckle, and TB broke into song. Country, of course, but still song and that was that. If the young horse leaned now it didn't matter, it would be something to talk about later over a large plate filled with steak, eggs, tomatoes and of course toast and coffee.

Trevor had finished the colt's trim quickly and without mishap, he knew that at some point in the last twenty-four hours all four of the young horse's legs would have been lifted, the soles patted and each leg would more than likely have spent a short amount of time tied up to a belly rope.

The old man firmly believed that individualism and bad manners should never use the other as an excuse. Horses were all great characters in their own right, yet they all had one thing in common: manners. They all, without exception, seemed to understand the acceptances rule. This is the basis of all forms of relationships between two or more players. It can be seen in any pack, or herd. It is in fact the social structure of every paddock and forest. So it seemed to the old man that, just because his pack was made up of different species, there was no reason for a lack of respect. Consequently he was surrounded by a sense of tranquillity, everybody knew the ground rules.

The stallion stood quietly as the farrier laid out his tools. As TB started to bend his back the horse would lift his closest leg and hold it steady. Trevor would cradle the hoof and get to work checking for any traces of seedy toe, making sure there were no soft areas that could conceal an abscess, putting on just enough pressure to ascertain that the internal structure of the sole was healthy and strong. During all of this the horse never moved.

"If only people would do the simple ground work," said Trevor, "this job would be so much easier. Then of course everybody would say, 'Why does the shoeing cost so much if you don't have to suffer?' Can't win, eh?"

The old man nodded and the farrier broke into song again. Later, sitting on the veranda having eaten steak and eggs and consumed numerous mugs of percolated coffee, the conversation got round to vermin and it was not long before they were discussing the events of the past week and the return of at least some of the feral pack.

"Do you reckon that old bitch has made it through another year?"

"Don't know," said the old man, "She wouldn't be easy to get rid of. Got a sixth sense that dog. Either that, or she has the luck of Jobe."

"They tell me the Prescott boys lost a good pig dog a month or so back. They said it must have been struck pretty bad for it not to come to call."

The old man digested Trevor's comment about the Prescott's dog.

"More coffee?"

"No, no," said Trevor as he got out of the chair, picking up his old worn Weathabeeta and his shoeing cap and throwing in the line, "Got to make the money to pay the tax man," put on his boots and started down the veranda steps.

The two men walked out to TB's four-wheel drive.

"I'll be back to shoe the colt."

"When's that?"

"After you call to say you're ready, that's when..."

"Well, that's when I'll see you then," said the old man, raising his hand as the Toyota drove out of the farm, leaving in its wake TB's rendition of, *Oh Lord, it's Hard to be Humble...*

The old man smiled at some quiet thought or other and headed towards the stables. The young horse still had his head collar on. He wasn't too sure about it the night before, when the man had introduced him to it. At the time he couldn't work out how it was suddenly on his neck. It had only been a second ago that he had stretched out his neck to smell it, as the old man offered it for his inspection and then, it was around his neck and over his nose. There seemed to be a small piece of something hanging down from his chin that followed wherever his head went, yet now, after only about eight hours, it was as if he had worn one all his life. Even the slight clang of the clip that joined the head-collar to the hanging catch-rope, as it caught on his water feeder, that the night before had made him jump back and tremble, was now just a part of his life.

How quickly the strangest and most fearsome of experiences need only the slightest familiarity to become the norm. The old man clipped a longer lead rope than would normally have been necessary onto the halter and with a certain amount of puffed up pomp from the colt they headed for the round yard.

The term is an obvious description of what it is. A yard that is round instead of square. The reason for the shape becomes more than obvious when you realise that in a round yard there are no corners. This means, of course, there is nowhere to hide, you can only sensibly go one way or another. And this is exactly what he did, walked round and round, with the old man standing in the middle of the circle watching and waiting. What for?

That moment of a slackening of pace, an ear changing direction, showing the first sign of query, that first realization that there could be more to life than just going in circles, that maybe the man in the middle should be checked out to see what effect, if any, he had to do with the situation at hand. After a rather feeble attempt at scaring himself and leaping forward, tucking in his rump and flicking his tail between his legs, he started to settle down.

Just when he was about to turn and see what the man was doing, he got a rude awakening. He suddenly discovered that the old man was hunting him; he was sending one end of the lead rope that though no longer attached to his halter, still seemed to be able to snake out towards him like an extension of the man's arm, actually pushing him to go faster. This was certainly not how things were meant to be. He lengthened his stride and changed his gait from rip-shit-and-bust to a floating extended trot, head up, neck stretched, his tail flowing behind him like a standard banner held aloft as the army charged into war. A more arrogant yet regal sight one would be hard pressed to find.

The man saw the near side ear flick backwards and centralise and rather like a ship's radar give the appearance of rotating, trying to seek out any sound that would give a clue as to the intentions of this friend or foe that seemed to occupy the same space as him. He knew that it would only be a matter of time before the young horse would stop and face him. He coiled up the long lead rope making no exaggerated movements, just quietly standing in the middle of a circle, watching the outer rim go round. It was sooner than he thought, that the horse stopped directly in front of him, squared himself and blew noisily out through his nostrils, standing defiant yet questioningly, facing the old man as if saying, 'Well, what now?'

He had wound up the extended rope while the colt had done his last two rounds of the yard and it hung loosely from his left hand. The colt shook his head but did not move his feet. The man smiled to himself and turning on his heel walked over to the gate, opened it and left the round yard closing the gate behind him. As he walked to the tack room he found himself whistling an old James Taylor song. He filled in the chorus with a soft rendition of *Good Night you Moonlit Ladies*, and *Rock a Bye Sweet Baby James.*

The horse took a step forward shaking his head. He really didn't know what to make of the situation. He had run on to get away from the man, yet the man hadn't moved, why not? He had slowed down and the man's long arm had flicked out behind him making him run faster, yet the man still hadn't moved. He stops and faces the man and says, 'Okay, let's do it your way, I'll face you and see who's who,' and the man walks away from him. Why didn't he want to talk? Why didn't he want to try to outrun him? If he had done that, he would have shown him a fair set of heels. He just walked away, why?

To work out this rather puzzling set of circumstances he needed to put his head in a corner and think. Now there arose an even bigger problem. All he could do was walk round and round. Somehow all the corners in his world seemed to have disappeared.

Later that afternoon the man had come back to the round yard carrying with him a bucket of clear spring fed water. He had put the bucket down and left the yard again. After a respectable lapse of time and a lot of safety sniffing the colt put his head down to the glistening liquid and drank long and noisily. Just before dusk, when the red streaks of tomorrow's promise were still vivid across the sky, the man came quietly to the yard and walked straight up to him, clipped a short lead rope to his halter and led him out of the gate and over to the stables. He followed without protest. He didn't know why, he just did.

He walked into the stable as if he had done so a hundred times before. The man slipped off the head collar and left the stable, closing top and bottom doors, leaving the colt once more alone. This was not the same stable that he had been in before. The smell was only of straw and fresh water and sweet Lucerne hay held up against the wall in a sort of a net. It all seemed so natural that after a hurried inspection of the bedding, a snort into the water bucket, he ended up in the position he liked most to stand in when thinking, and that of course was a corner. So there he stood, slowly nibbling away at the contents of the hay net and ruminating on the days' occurrences.

SEVEN
A Kill

In the early hours of the morning the big hound had come across the bitch's scent. He had followed it along the ledge, lost it at her jump rock, traversed back and forth, nose glued to the ground till he found it again. He came to the cave's entrance, stopped and inhaled deeply, dissecting the odours from within; his highly tuned senses told him that she was not in residence, a shame, as her trail had been interesting, not so much the pungent smell of a bitch in season, yet there was still a come hither type of call to it.

He detected another scent wafting out of the cave's entrance, a neutral, soft, fudgy, milky smell. He edged forward slowly, moving only his front legs, stretching his neck out to its fullest extent, opening his incredibly sensitive nostrils, and deciphering the interior's secrets. His back legs were ready to react depending on the attitude of the occupant. There was no aggressive reaction to his move and as his hindquarters moved slowly closer, he entered the bitch's den.

Her head came up with start, water dripping from her outstretched tongue. It had been a hard fast chase, she had literally jogged onto the feeding paddy melon, both animals caught unawares. The paddy melon, being a marsupial similar in size to a small wallaby, had reacted with a massive leap for its size and had the advantage of initial flight, with head stretched to maximum length and back legs thrusting away like pistons. If the bitch had not had the pups to feed she would probably have let this speedy little muscular fur ball go on its merry way, but nature and instinct came into play and the bitch was off in hot pursuit. The small marsupial had the distinct advantage of two extra strides on the dog and the determination of survival, unfortunately it had misjudged the creek crossing and had landed badly, which was all the bitch needed to gain the upper hand, landing on top of the paddy melon, knocking the air from its pumping lungs and grasping its throat all in the same motion.

Dragging her kill onto the bank, she had gone back to the water and lain in the creek and lapped greedily at the fresh clear liquid as it rushed past, then suddenly the hair on her neck rose up and she tensed; there was no apparent reason for her action, no loud noise to give her cause for alarm, yet here she was; her attention focused on an invisible event, somewhere she should be, and it wasn't here.

The meal that only seconds ago was of prime importance was now discarded as she leaped from the creek onto the bank and was in full stride the minute her feet touched dry land. There was no fear in her as she approached her den, only a mother's courage; she had no clue as to why she had this feeling of foreboding as she entered the cave, lips back, teeth bared, legs and tail stiff, ready for action of any kind.

Her confusion was understandable; she tried to curl herself around each pup so they may feed, nosing them closer together, try as she may, she could not change the fact that the two inert bodies were now cold, the puppy smell had faded already and all that was left were the two forms, lying apart where they had landed after the hound had worried and shaken them. The hound had soon lost interest, he relieved himself at the cave' entrance and without giving a second thought to the now spent lives, loped off easily into the pre-dawn light.

The bitch knew nothing of the event that had taken place here in the confines of her den, only that what was, was no more. Grieving time in the wild never interrupts survival, she gave the two lifeless little forms a final nudge, a last push, just to verify they were not sleeping then she turned her back on the cave's interior and went out into the morning sun.

EIGHT
Talking Begins

What makes the world go round? It can't just be money, as the song says, surely there must be more to it than that. He sat on the veranda and pondered the question, it had always amused him the way that certain people played the game, those who considered their persona so important that they managed to disregard everybody else's opinions with ease. He hit the switch and the radio became a piece of object d'art instead of a direct line to world news. "Heh, Heh," he said quietly to himself, could this be company come for some intrusive play? The red dog growled deep inside her throat and positioned herself just in front of the man as he rose from the chair.

"Steady, there's no need for that, girl."

The land rover came to a halt in a cloud of dust and the occupant started his tirade of objections before his feet hit the ground, his reasons for them and of course the most important factor, it's the only way to-do it, I'm telling you, he then spun around, walked back to the four wheel drive and left with a tirade of muttering about fools not knowing how to farm.

The old man looked down at the red dog and stroked her head in an absentminded fashion. Manners maketh man, they used to say, that self-centred megalomaniac should get himself a government grant to learn some,

"Well, old girl, somebody must have told him I didn't want my lemon trees poisoned, he'll be after killing the jacarandas soon."

The old man didn't really have much time for the do-gooders who used the grant system to empire build whilst at the same time telling all and sundry what an amazing job they were doing for the community.

"We've got better things to do with our time, haven't we girl," he laughed, putting the rude and uninvited visitor out of sight and out of mind.

Being a traveller of circumstance and opportunity the old man had an insight into action and reaction, in simple terms all it meant was, he looked further than the obvious. There was usually an underlying agenda that at the very least involved money, and in most cases, government grants, of which at least forty percent ended up being spent in administration. It was a great way to make living if you had enough huff and puff to confuse those who might object. This was in most cases done by holding a very well stacked public meeting and if there were any objections then a quick blustering visit, which could be called intimidating if only because it was all bluster and bad manners.

Then again, one gets used to bullies as one's life goes through the stages of development or your education into what was also commonly called progress.

The two horses had stood with their heads in the same corner, separated only by the width of a timber flitch for five days now. When the colt left his stable in the morning for the round yard the stallion was still locked up. As the colt spent most of his day in the round yard, he had no idea when the stallion left his stable, only that he was not there when he came back, but would arrive much later when it was dark. Each night the man would say the same thing,

"Let me cross the straps over, thank you, well, that's you done, get into your feed and I'll see you in the morning. Oh, and if you feel like it, have a chat to your protégée, he's next door, but you knew that, didn't you?"

There would be the sound of a hand on canvas sliding along the material slowly and all the time tapping with long slender fingers, then the final double pat, good night my son, the stable door top and bottom were closed and the lights went out as soon as the bolt was drawn across the double doors, a nightly ritual that ensured warmth and security for the occupant inside.

Outside it was one of those balmy nights where a wind change had occurred and the day's heat had been reduced to a rather polite pre-chill. As he headed towards the veranda there could be heard the soulful voice of Otis Redding strutting out an era that had influenced the old man's awareness in many ways. That was the good thing about cd players, you could set them to start at any time, so that you could always pre-set the atmosphere that you think you might like, and therefore plan your veranda's greeting to suit.

As the old man sank into his favourite chair the sweet sound of *Sitting on the dock of the bay* wafted its way down to the two locked stables. The most prominent sensation to both the horses was the bass, which the man usually had fractionally louder than most.

The colt had got to the stage with his hay net that one could only call pre-limbo time. It's that point where eating is no longer of prime importance, yet sleep has not quite taken over, a time were the slightest twitch of the top lip made a protruding Lucerne stem become the instrument of exquisite pleasure. Not only did it tickle the soft and incredibly sensitive area that he would normally use as a sifting and sorting tool, it also gave him a sensation that invoked drowsiness -a bit like a child and its comfort blanket. It was in the middle of one of these twitches, just as he was entering the void between consciousness and dream, that he first heard it. There it was again!

"Colt." Louder this time.

He skittered on all fours, head up, eyes wide, nostrils flared, sucking in the night air, sifting through the smell of his stable, its timber surrounds, the sweet smelling Lucerne, the grain in the stallion's feed bin next door, the stallion…. The stallion!

'Not possible,' he said to himself.

There had been no interaction between them since his arrival.

Hah. Once again the voice boomed out. Well, well, braced and ready for action, bravery or bluff, it could be either, the colt dropped his stance and searched around him as he stood in the middle of the stable.

In the next-door stable the old campaigner knew by the sounds that filtered through the slab walls exactly where the colt was standing. He could hear his heart beating even faster now. Also there was a change in smell. Agitation and confusion, also a little trepidation, probably because it appeared to him that his safety had become his prison.

"The Princess seems to believe that you are the one".

"One what?" The words came quickly and without thought.

"The one who will keep his pride, the one that will carry on the line of his forbears. Not a gelding, not a total servant, to accept without reason. Not as the Romans made eunuchs for strength and servitude, yet posing no danger of passing on their bloodlines, therefore posing no threat to the maidens in the father's paddock."

"Who is the father?" said the colt.

In a tone that would suggest that the stallion was talking to himself out loud, the colt heard his ruminations.

"He answers too quickly to have given adequate thought, yet he bypassed the story and went straight to the point, straight to the crux, straight to survival. Maybe the Princess is right. It has been so long…"

"What?" screamed the colt.

"Manners maketh man, boy. There is no difference in our culture. Learn some."

Then there was silence. The colt knew that he would itch in the morning, as he could feel the increasing chill in the air dry the dampness of his coat, leaving lines of salt swathed across his rump and down his shoulder. That was all that was left of his first encounter with the old stallion, even the music had stopped and the only light that was filtering through the cracks in the slab walls was from the star-filled night.

It was barely dawn when the old man saddled up the stallion and headed off the following morning. The colt heard them leave and by the time the yard was empty he was awake enough to realize that his last thought of the night before was indeed quite correct, for itch he did. His coat started to ripple and twitch not like a clear running stream; it was more like the movement of the hardy skin of a solitary old bull as he resigns himself to the fact that the continual swishing of his tail never reached far enough and would never stop the buffalo fly from its incessant attack. His skin had tightened due to the congealed salt pulling at his hairs, his twitching was continuous, and unbelievably irritating.

Meanwhile, the stallion was striding along the lane. He could walk out at ten to twelve km an hour without the slightest stress and he enjoyed the freedom to do so. The man sat deep in the saddle, looking to all intents and purpose as if he was part of the horse. He could see one of his neighbours in the distance looking up the hill with a pair of binoculars. Squeezing ever so gently on the stallion's sides with his legs, he gave his friend the signal for an increase in his pace, not breaking into a trot, just lengthening his stride a fraction. As he got closer to the dairy farmer, one of the very few left in the area after deregulation, he noticed that the collie kelpie cross that was usually glued to the farmer's heel by an invisible thread, was lying, flat out on the back of the Ute, with no apparent movement. As he got closer, he saw the dog was still breathing, if only faintly. But on closer inspection from his vantage point, he also saw the large gashes around the dog's neck and one leg which at first glance appeared to be badly mangled.

"She doesn't look too good," said the old man.

"Bloody isn't!" Was the dairy farmer's reply, "I found her in the Springer paddock next to a dead calf that's given something a good feed. I saw dogs up near the tree line, they'll be long gone by now."

"Did you get a decent look at them?" asked the old man as he dismounted and let the reins drop to the ground.

"Not really. I only saw two, but I'll tell you what. The lead dog seemed a big bugger and that's for sure."

"Not that rogue bitch then. I had a feeling she might be back," said the old man as he affectionately cuffed the stallion, who was tugging on his jacket pocket.

Without seemingly taking any notice of the man's objection, the horse kept hold of the pocket and closing his eyes, just lent against his friend.

"I didn't take much notice of the second dog. The lead dog sort of grabbed my attention, big rangy sort of beast with a head on him like; well I don't really know what to compare it to. It was just big."

The old man tapped the stallion on the shoulder and the horse edged his front legs forward, leaving the back ones where they stood. Putting his foot into the stirrup he mounted easily and the horse altered his stance accordingly.

"If that horse makes your life any easier, he'll be able to apply for a carer's pension," laughed the farmer.

The old man chuckled,

"I love him dearly, but I don't think I would want him tucking me into bed each night."

Shaking his head, the stallion reminded the old man that there were things to do, and places to go, they turned into the slope leading to the tree line,

"I'll phone you tonight if I come across anything." And they strode away.

I will just check the mare's paddock, he thought to himself before going home. Reaching the trees he swung onto the old bullock track that the loggers had used to drag down timber from the high country years ago, and they melted into the tree line and disappeared from sight.

The colt heard them return and then he heard the hose start to splutter and the stallion blew out loudly. It was at least another half hour before the top door of his stable opened and the mid-morning light flooded in. The stallion must be in his day paddock, as he had not come back to his stable.

Even though it had only been a few days, he had got used to the comings and goings of the man and the stallion. This change in routine and the events of the night before made him feel a little tense and uneasy.

"Well my lad, what's upset you?" said the man as he saw the sweat marks lining the young colt's sides.

"We'd better wash you down before we do anything else."

Now the old man's routine was out of place as this was the time he usually sat for a while on the veranda with a much enjoyed cup of coffee as he planned his day. 'Not a drama,' he thought to himself. The percolator would keep the coffee hot and the young horse would be much more comfortable after a wash down.

The two dogs were charging backward and forward along the bank of the dam, every third or fourth bound became a huge leap upwards as they tried to catch the dragonflies that hovered over their heads. They had met up two days prior and as there was no bitch around to fight over, they had after much stiff legged, hair-raised, circling and general sniffing, marked a tuft of grass, both dogs covering and re-covering their last attempts, mutually agreeing that the hound was the lead dog of the two and like any two bachelors, if there are no members of the opposite sex about, came to the same conclusion, let's go hunting. And they had.

Their first mayor kill had been a new born calf. They had come across the cow in the middle of the paddock under a shade tree just as she slipped out the afterbirth - and the rest is history. The collie had just been one of those things, it really didn't matter whether she wanted to protect the calf or steal it from them. The hound didn't bother to ask, he just treated her as an enemy.

The hound's newfound friend was one of the dogs that had been on the chicken raid. Then, when the pack had split up on the stallion's territorial ledge, he and another young dog had run themselves ragged. They had run along the top of the ridge and rather than take the long way round the main peak, they had chosen to climb straight up and over the top of the rocky escarpment. And being the younger of the two, he had followed without question.

The lesson the young dog learnt that day was less haste more speed. The front-runner carried straight on, covering the comparatively flat ground in no time at all and disappeared over what appeared to be just another large rock. This was, in fact, the edge of a small precipice, which would have presented very little trouble to a strong dog at an average lope, but the usual breaking method does not work on shale, which is what the dog came across, only six paces from the top. Once the perpetual motion called slide starts on a shale base, it has the same effect as a vertical glacier. Nothing stops the forward movement. So, as the dog was hurled out into infinity, the younger dog, who had only just arrived at the large rock, just lay down amongst the soft grassy tufts panting at an exaggerated rate waiting for the right time to swallow and so reduce his over-heating. This action is probably what saved his life.

The fact that his travelling companion of the night before was now an ever-fading memory did not bother him. He was more intent on finding a reliable source of water and hopefully a meal of some description to replace some of his expended energy.

So it was not surprising that he and the older hound had crossed paths, and here they were playing at the water's edge like puppies on an outing; then again nothing is ever as it seems.

NINE
Further Conversations

The colt's day in the round yard had been quite a shambles. He could not concentrate, he did not listen and rather than call it a bad lesson, the old man left him in the round yard to sort himself out and get his attitude together. No point in fighting, it was always better to be the saviour than the aggressor. He retired to the veranda, feet up on the balustrade and enjoyed the much-welcome coffee that he had forgone earlier.

Looking at the red dog and the wall-eyed bitch as they lay spread out on the timber floors, he decided that to really appreciate what one has, it is sometimes necessary to remind oneself of what others have not got. Not that he ever needed to justify to anyone any of his actions. The days of others needing him to explain a simple action because they had nothing better in their lives to do than criticise and object, had passed.

He just enjoyed thinking of all the justifications he could think of, if indeed his home situation may become different; every tick of the clock brought the unknown closer. The one thing he did not need was to become philosophical, so chuckling, he hit the remote and the world news took over the television screen.

The talk of Bin Laden and of September eleventh had a reduced impact on people now, it was a memory with only anniversaries as the news items had moved on to world terrorism, local fires and the addition of millions to the millions already starving.

The television went back to that delightful shade of off and as his fingers dallied across the rows of CD's, John Lennon seemed to leap into his hands and by the time he had started down the veranda stairs, *Imagine* was already playing.

The stallion was in his day yard and he knew, as soon as he heard the music start, that his cohort in life would soon be joining him for his afternoon rub. The conversation, as always, would be the man talking, the stallion listening, occasionally nodding his head and, or swishing his tail, just to let the man know that he was listening. Of course there were times when the sheer bliss of the brush, as it travelled across his coat, removing any tiny perpetrators, combined with the lyrical softness of the man's voice, made concentration often hard.

This day, this day was different. The conversation was all centred on the colt, his ability to listen, learn, to take note, to be aware, most importantly, to be worthy. This long and often lyrical reasoning, this ode to the Libran's logic, waxed and waned between rejecting keeping the colt a prince among princes and acceptance that the good qualities out-weighed the rest. And the old man considered the colt's apparent lack of interest during the morning session, even down to the vague possibility that the change in his attitude may have been the addition of an extra wash down, which naturally had entailed extra walking, extra grooming and all of that before going to the round yard. Had he maybe been too judgemental, was he continuing to be? This carried on over the space of approximately two hours or more. The stallion had the whole story from beginning to end, with every justification possibly known to man, if not more.

Later that night, when the man had retired and all had calmed to the normal sounds of the night-time inhabitants of the farm, the stallion did not mince his words. If the colt could not come to terms with what he was about to impart, then the old man would be right - he did not in fact command the qualities of a prince.

"We are from the King of Kings," he began.

The colt was immediately awake, as he had only been in half limbo. The gravity in the old stallion's voice held the colt spellbound.

"Our dams are the Princesses elite. There was no country known that the Arab had not been to, that he had not conquered. From the burning desert, to the mountains of the American Rockies, and wherever he went they all knew him by his high tail carriage, arched neck and a high stepping arrogance that, if asked to, would be backed to the hilt with barred teeth and swift retribution."

The sheer beauty of his persona changing radically as the ears went back and the face took on the visage of judgement day, a fearful sight in anyone's eyes.

"No hill too steep, no mountain too high, no prairie too desolate, no desert too dry, no distance too great, to endure, to survive with dignity and flair, to take pride in one's very being, to flaunt and accept its responsibilities.

"The Arab's natural flair was for all others to enjoy in whatever way they may choose and for those of our culture who, through no fault of their own, are less fortunate than we. Horses with no sense of self - just herd horses, nondescript, to be ruled over.

"And when they meet their mythical time and frolic in harmony watched over by Pegasus and the unicorns, they will remember us and know that the secret is still passed on. That is what our heritage is, and for us to live up to. It is for you to do. It can either be your very heart and soul, or it can be your ball and chain. The choices are yours and yours alone.

"Man only takes away what you are prepared to give, no matter what part of you is lost to the knife."

"Ball and chain," said the colt, "What ball and chain?"

"Later," said the stallion with an abruptness that would silence the most interruptive of youngsters,

"Just listen. Your dam, the princess, is connected to our lineage through assignations during and after a great war. The lineage on her side was magnificent in stature, a power so great that there was no knight in armour that they could not take into battle with mighty strides and carry till all was won or lost. There was no weight that was known to them that they could not pull, no ground too hard for them to till, even if it meant the joining of many strengths.

"They were one of the backbones of the food chain across many worlds; their gentility was second to none, and their strength and sheer determination to succeed made them kings and queens in their own culture on a par to our own."

This time there was a very long silence, and then the colt spoke,

"And?" "What do you mean? Well, there has to be more," said the colt; "You wouldn't have placed so much importance on where we come from if you weren't concerned as to where we are going."

'Again he does it to me, straight to the point,' the stallion pondered over the colt's statement, half thinking aloud.

"We," he said, "is the wrong word. I, already am, you are yet to be." … A much shorter silence this time.

"Please sir, can you explain yourself more clearly," said the colt.

"I would have thought," said the stallion, "that it was obvious: a flashy springy colt does not always make a suitable prince. It does not mean that just because you are from this incredible lineage that you are worthy of its continuation; a true prince needs to be able to concentrate, to apply himself to the task at hand, to show aptitude, and common sense.

"We with Arab blood lines also carry the cross of being dizzy in the head - a little crazy perhaps - mainly because of man's ineptitude to cull properly as a herd stallion would normally do. The strongest and most capable of colts follow the line of their kings and queens; this does not necessarily mean the prettiest or flashiest, for gloss does not always equate with brains, or strength, or the ability to lead."

Now the colt was stumped for words. He had always taken for granted that the reflection he had seen in the still, deep areas of the river was of perfection, that the way his blood flowed through his veins at different speeds depending on his circumstances, was attributed to valour, yet here he was being told that there was more to life than just the sheer joy of living.

The stallion continued,

"Beauty is in the eye of the beholder, the tenacity to live and overcome life's twists and turns with dignity and self-confidence comes from within."

A longer silence followed, then,

"I will try to explain in a way that makes it easier for you to understand; through examples, if you like. For instance, imagine standing in a paddock full of clover and looking at the next paddock, seeing only the oat tops, mild and sweet. Once the fence or hedge separating the two areas has been bested, and access to this field of plenty is allowed, then there may be a puzzle to fathom. For the paddock further on looks even greener, and the paddock you just came from looks even greener still.

"Why, you might ask? … As I was saying, you had taken for granted where you were, and only upon following greed, instead of calculation and common sense, did you see what you had missed. The moral being, where you were in the first place, was where you were supposed to be."

Silence once again reigned supreme.

"Some form of expressing the fact that you are still awake and not just standing there in total sleep mode, would be a luxury I don't suppose you could afford, mm?" The stallion snorted.

"You told me to listen and not to speak," said the colt, in a slightly too defiant tone.

"A polite sire will do! I don't think it is necessary to add lack of respect to a lack of civility. Now, where was I going?

"Now, greed in this sense was the eyes seeing only the sweet tops, and nothing else, so without further thought you followed a basic instinct, greed, to gorge, there is no judgment placed on this action, this is a basic necessity to achieve the continuation of your survival, the field of plenty."

It was at this point that the stallion decided to take time out for himself; and being himself, he stretched out his neck, twisting his head to one side and yawned, not just your average, Oh, how boring sort of yawn, this was one of the major jaw bone stretching exercises , followed with a toss of the head, then a shake, half a blow through the nostrils, and then straight to the water supply in the corner of the stable… a long-drawn out series of loud sucking noises and another blow - a full-on cleansing of the nasal passages, then back to fiddling with the surface of the water using only the velvet part of his top lip..

The colt was nearly beside himself with frustration; he had to exercise an enormous amount of control not to make any unnecessary noise, let alone blurt out the questions that so noisily rushed around his head.

The stallion raised his head and the colt heard the drops of water as they fell back into the container.

"There was once a young prince," the stallion blew out this time very noisily, then, having cleared his nasal passages thoroughly, continued…

"Who, after serious discussions with his sire - which meant that he was chased out with many nips and bites to his rump and other parts that his sire could get to - as he unceremoniously and in much confusion fled.

"He was being forcibly ousted from the herd as all young colts were, once they reached a certain age. That meant leaving his dam, who was paying all her attention to this year's little filly, the prince's younger sister.

"To go in search of his own territory seemed like a very good idea. There had been much stamping of feet, arching of necks and squealing, but no really serious damage had been done, and the prince had seen reason before the stallion had needed to resort to a full-on attack, which involves much more than just teeth and nips. This is the next move taken when instructing a headstrong colt on the laws of the herd.

"After getting over his chagrin, he wandered for many days, coming across signs that indicated the movement of large numbers of his own kind. Yet look as he might, he never found them.

"Then one day as he was traversing the side of a particularly steep incline, he noticed that there was a hidden valley below that the gully went into, which looked incredibly lush and green, with permanent water from a spring that gushed out of the side of the ravine. There were also the most uniquely set and impenetrable shade trees.

"He could not for the life of him see a way out, except of course to go back along the narrow gully floor. It was a dead end that nature had created; it was man that had turned it into the trap that it now was.

"As he followed the ridge along, it became apparent that the mouth of the gully was actually very wide, opening out into a great plain covered in a variety of foods. Here was freedom, space, and unlike the hidden valley behind him, an area with no boundaries. Total freedom, this was the place for him.

"Turning his back to the valley with no horizon, he leapt forward, giving an incredibly high buck and several long side kicks and then settled into an exaggerated trot, his head high, neck extended, nostrils open wide, sucking in all the air his lungs could contain, sifting through the scent trails eagerly awaiting the possibility of the smell of something that he would recognise as another horse, for surely in this land of plenty there must be another of his kind."

The stallion shook his head, stamped a front foot, yawned, and became as a statue; no movement whatsoever, not even the slightest twitch of the ear. To make matters worse he was silent; the colt was beside himself once again, only this time he said nothing and the night was his only companion, for the stallion was to all intents and purposes, fast asleep.

TEN
Lessons Learned

As usual, the old man woke early and by the time the sun had successfully spread its smile across the countryside he was enjoying the delights of his second cup of freshly brewed coffee. From his vantage point on the veranda he could survey the farmyard and its many and varied outbuildings, knowing his immediate surroundings so intimately that he could tell at a glance if all was well, which it was. That meant that his day was starting calmly and all was at peace. He noticed that the resident male peacock was frantically showing off to the chickens, who naturally were about as interested as a dead ferret, if you will forgive the expression. They entertained themselves in their normal way, pecking and sorting over the manure pile.

During all this the peacock strutted his stuff, spreading his tail feathers and rattling the quills. 'I must check the pea hen's usual hiding places,' the man thought to himself - just in case she was sitting. It always amused him to watch the peacock trying to entice a chook; he normally only attempted to round up the chickens if his hens were busy sitting.

The old man picked up the now empty coffee cup and headed for the kitchen; today would be a very good day - he could feel it in his step and in the air.

Within the hour Himself was saddled, bridled, and the two old friends were well away from the farm proper and heading steadily upward, turning from time to time and looking outward at the valley below. It never ceased to amaze him how beautiful

Australia was, and this part of the North Eastern corner of NSW was certainly no exception, from the secluded valleys to the panoramic views, only accessible by a hard test of fitness for both animal and man alike.

Apart from the stockmen and occasional government person, the only other people to travel in these wilds of the country were the endurance riders and then only two or three times a year, always along well planned routes accessible to the local fire truck pulling along behind, in case it was needed at any time. Also on these ventures came the horse float, commonly called a rescue float just in case a horse had a bad fall or a rider suffered from dehydration and collapsed on track. It was an insurance necessity that all ride tracks had to have this form of accessibility to comply with the complex rules of the endurance scene.

To arrive at the top ridge, Himself and the old man both enjoyed a sense of exhilaration. For the horse it was the sheer joy of putting his head down and sampling grasses not found in the valley, then putting his head up and catching all the smells from far and wide. The little pockets of water were enough to sate his thirst, for they had stopped at two of the dams on the way up.

As for the old man, for him just to lean on a rock and look out and away was one of his biggest joys. He knew of the different smells drifting past on the breeze just by watching the stallion's reactions; the sudden movement of his head, the rearranging of his ears and the dilation of his nostrils. He always loved to watch him dissecting the wind; it was as if he had his own early warning system: through the stallion he could tell the difference between the movement of a startled Roo, and a change in the weather not yet noticeable to the naked eye. He could share that special unity with nature just by being with his friend.

It was such a shame that so many people nowadays had never been made aware of the pure magic of our planet - instead, the world seemed bent on disregarding its basic essence - Mother Earth.

The silence was broken by a small flock of black cockatoos screeching raucously as they flew overhead, being at a vantage point that allowed him to see for miles and miles in any direction, he noticed that there were a number of clouds mainly shaped like puff balls beginning to form in the east. Storms or even the vague possibility of rain had not been a feature in the early morning weather report yet the black cockatoos seemed to think differently, he spoke softly to the stallion who fluttered his nostrils in response and together they started their descent back down to the valley below, he walking just ahead of the stallion, the reins resting on his shoulder. As they got closer to the valley floor, the temperature change was quite dramatic, gone was that wonderful freshness of mountain air and as the humidity started to rise, the day took on a different feel.

Himself was aware of the fact that not once had the old man mentioned the prince, that could only mean one thing, that today was the day, the day when he would make his judgement: prince or servant. He would hear more when his friend came in to rug him later on before the cool change came creeping in, which meant that he would dally for as long as he wanted, as it would be the last thing that the man would do before climbing the veranda steps and into the other world of music and dreams that he lived in.

He had put the young colt in the round yard before hosing down the stallion and had retired to the veranda for a short repose as the cooler southerly came in, as was its way at this time in the afternoon, a blessed relief from the heat of the day and a good time to work the young colt. It always amazed him how quickly time elapsed when he and the stallion went a-venturing; how people managed to keep their sanity in big cities was a mystery to him. The hustle and bustle was bad enough, but the total disregard for their fellow man made him feel that people had totally lost any camaraderie that they once might have had.

He looked down at the two dogs at his feet,

"Well girls," he said, and two tails in unison thumped the floor, "Why don't you come to the round yard and let's see how this young colt behaves today, what do you think?"

The old man got out of his chair and started towards the steps, instantly there were two dogs at his heels, he smiled and the trio headed across the yard to the tack room.

The old man entered the round yard; it was as if he had been transported into another world. The yard was constructed of wooden flitches or slabs as some refer to them, half rounds also fit the bill, that when slotted sideways into rounds of at least twelve inches creates an area where nothing outside should affect or distract its occupants.

The old man stood in the middle of this solid and un-jumpable circle, two dogs lying down three feet away from him, one on either side; in his gloved right hand was a coiled rope. His head looked down at the ground and there was a relaxed air in his demeanour, his movements, direct in their intention yet in no way threatening. He seemed no longer the old man, he was more a part of nature, an owner of territory, the king of the round yard, not to be questioned, never to be ignored.

In the wild, the head stallion would control all, and the colt was about to recognise the fact that here was the head stallion he had to follow. He would have to concentrate, and not just for a second or two, for his future in whatever capacity it may be, would all be decided in probably the next hour.

The dogs lay with their heads stretched out towards their paws, the only movement being their eyes as they followed the man's movements. If you looked closely you would see that the relaxed and seemingly disinterested dogs were in fact covering every step made by the man, their hind quarters tensed in fine tune, they knew exactly the time it would take to be wherever they were asked to go, and on command, and at what speed to travel.

The colt had been intrigued with the two dogs, going towards them both in turn, first the red dog, stretching out his neck and snorting. Even though he got no reaction, he pre-empted the possibility of an attack, and jumped immediately away, then with head down puffing up little flurries of dust, slowly headed over to the wall-eyed dog, who like her maidenly sister, except for a silent raising of her lips, ignored him completely.

This in turn fascinated him as he knew the dogs only as passers-by, now they were right here, with him, inside this place with no corners. He was so preoccupied with this fact that he did not at first realise that he was being herded. Instead of doing what he had been, which was taking two bounds away from one dog and then sauntering over to the other, all of a sudden he had kept going, and was trotting around the yard. He was going round and round and now as he realised what was happening, at a slightly increased speed, yet still going absolutely nowhere and rather quickly at that. The dogs never moved and he just went round and round, his neck arched high and proud legs thrown straight out with great exaggeration in front of him making him appear longer and larger and so much stronger, nostrils flared, ears set in the permanently forward position.

The man, of course, had not moved from his original position between the two dogs, and there he stood watching, once again for that sign, that single twitch of the ear closest to him, the slightest relaxing of a muscle.

The colt started to slow down, trying to take control of his own pace. The extended arm in the form of the rope snaked out and landed just behind him; he leapt forward and once again he knew he was being pushed. It irked him more than just a little, so that this time, as if to prove a point, he went even faster, yet still he got nowhere, and the dogs never moved and neither did the form in the middle. He just looked at the ground and completely ignored the colt altogether.

The young prince began to realise that the only thing inside the place with no corners who was agitated was him, and he started looking around to find the reason why. The form in the middle wasn't even looking at him, and the two dogs couldn't care less, so why was he running? He started to slow down, gradually reducing his now more than energetic canter to a more sedate trot, and finally a sort of amble. The man looked up and the colt increased his walk a fraction to a good pace, yet not in any way too hurried. The man gave a low whistle and the red bitch got up and slowly started to trot round on a smaller circle adjacent to the horse. Another whistle preceded by a click that he made by pulling his tongue sharply away from the roof of his mouth. He had first heard the sound in Africa about forty years ago and adopted it as a call sign.

The wall-eyed collie cross rose instantly and took up a position slightly behind the red dog and closer by half to the colt, padding along at same speed as the other dog. Even when the colt increased his pace a fraction the dogs never wavered from theirs; always right there, trotting along at the same rate. And when he dropped back, he still had to stay in front of the dogs, keeping the pace that they set which was on command from the man in the middle.

It wasn't long before the colt accepted the fact that the dogs were there, they didn't inhibit his movements and they stayed out of kick range. They just padded along, then there was a low whistle and the dogs returned to their central position next to the man; the colt started to slow down and once again out snaked the extended arm, the colt increased his pace and continued to circle round and round.

The man seemed pleased; the atmosphere in the enclosed yard was in no way threatening, there was a feeling of unity: the man, the dogs, and a young prince. The colt's ear moved towards the man as if waiting for the next move, he had started to listen. The next hour was magical to watch, the four of them becoming a team, joined, and receptive, getting to know, accept, and trust each other. This for no other reason than their close proximity and the fact that there was no one else; so trust each other they must, and they trusted because they could.

The old man was very pleased with how the day had gone, horse wise, that is. And it showed, not only in his choice of music, he had also lit his cigar earlier than usual, and was enjoying a strong black coffee and a dash of whisky, this simple concoction was then heavily sugared. Terribly bad for one, but it isn't every day that things just sort of slip into place and then pan out so well. Next to it was the obligatory glass of iced water with a slice of lemon that he always had with strong coffee. The sigh that gently followed was one of contentment more than anything else, for tonight he was truly at peace with his immediate and quite satisfactory world.

Down at the stables, the stallion having heard not only the *Rolling Stones* version of *Walking the dog*, but also *Wilson Pickett's*, as the speakers, which were turned up much higher than usual, wafted their tones down into the farm yard.

"My friend is very happy tonight," he said, more to himself than to the colt in the next stable, but the young prince was eager to get back into conversation. It had been the longest and most frustrating time for him, since the stallion had fallen asleep in mid-thought the night before.

"How do you know?" asked the colt.

"Mmm," said the stallion," a little taken aback that his private conversation had been heard.

"If you used your ears, then you would know,"

"How?"

"By opening them for starters. Listen! Can't you hear the music, that noise that fills the night and drowns out even the most persistent of frogs croaking?"

"Of course I can, it would be hard not to," said the frustrated young colt.

"Well then, it is that noise that takes him back in time, it makes him smile, it makes him remember things, things that touch his spirit deep inside, that which is part of his wildness. It is not only our kind that has been touched by things - friends, times and places, good and bad, they all have a memory within, and at special times they come out and into one's mind and let us drift and sway within their sweetness or their sorrow. And this is obviously a special time; that is how I know."

"Oh," said the colt, "what is so special about today?"

The old stallion took a deep and meaningful breath and then said,

"I am of the opinion that it might have something to do with you, or, whatever happened between you and him this afternoon. Well! Speak boy, or is your brain so addled, or so tired that you don't know what you did today? Talk to me, give me something to mull over - something of meaning."

"What did I do?" said the befuddled colt. "Well, I spent a long time in the yard with no corners."

"Fox and squint, were they there?"

"The dogs? Yes, they were there."

"And?"

"And, what?" The colt was mystified; he did not have the faintest idea what the stallion was talking about.

"What did you do in the yard with no corners?"

"I ran," said the colt. "I ran."

"Why?" mused the stallion. "Tell me why. Because there was nowhere to go, you ran because there was nowhere to go? Except of course round in circles?"

A long silence ensued, "Well!" said the stallion, with the beginnings of exasperation. "That really makes sense."

"Well, it did at the time;" said the young colt, who was now becoming even more confused, and more than a little upset, because as with all young and proud creatures, he hated to feel stupid, especially when he didn't know exactly why he felt that way.

"If it is not too much of a strain, I would appreciate it if you could try to recall the events after you stopped running nowhere in particular?"

The colt tried very hard to gather his thoughts and put them into sequence; he snorted, stamped his foot as if to clear the way for an oration. He started off slowly at first, picking his words with deliberation.

"The man, forgive me, your friend, stood in the middle of the yard with no corners, the two dogs sat close by, once I realised that no harm was meant towards me, I slowed down.

"When his long arm came out behind me I was surprised, no, it was more that I was a little frightened, and a little scared that he could get so close from so far away. So, I went faster, then the dogs came out and the red one ran next to me but out of my kick range and the dog with the one blue eye ran behind me."

"Ah, ha," said the stallion, "He was obviously looking to see if you could concentrate on more than one thing at a time. Now, just try to cast your mind back to the story of the headstrong young colt that had gone off on his own to discover a world where he and he alone could rule.

"Do you remember the track down the escarpment to the valley below and how he had noticed there was no other way out from that valley, except to retrace his steps? Well if you recall, he had started out into the wide plains area to find company of his own kind."

This was what he had wanted to hear about, not the whys and wherefores of the yard with no corners. All he wanted to know was what was going to happen to the young colt now that he was heading outward onto the plains, and a new life, freedom and space.

The stallion repaid his patience by continuing:

"He had, after what seemed like an eternity, come across the smell of something that could possibly be of interest. A strange sort of smell, neither stallion or mare, nor colt or filly, yet still of his kind… There was no gender reference, just neutral. He blew out his nostrils and shook himself lightly, heading towards the smell of water that he had detected on the incoming breeze.

"On reaching the small stream, he put his nose down and drank deeply from the swiftly running rivulet. He then raised his head, water dripping from his mouth, then he surveyed his immediate surroundings. Nothing seemed out of the ordinary, except, except, there was another of his kind up stream, looking straight at him. He arched his neck and flared his nostrils, stamping the ground with his front feet. Yet the horse upstream totally ignored the challenge, instead with a casual flick of the tail and the faintest sound of a nicker, possibly a greeting, had just turned his back on him and walked away.

"The young stallion was confused; he did not know if he had just won a battle or been disregarded as an unworthy opponent. He gave a half rear and screamed at the now retreating horse with no positive scent."

Himself took a breath and the young prince could not contain his questions any longer.

"What do you mean, no scent, why couldn't the stallion work out if the horse was a mare, or a filly, or whatever?"

The old stallion cut him short,

"Try to wait until you have all the facts before you ask questions, otherwise all that will happen is you will never hear everything you should have. Try listening to what is being said or you will never learn anything at all."

"Why?" said the prince and the stallion sighed mightily as if he was thinking what is the point?

He slowly let his head sink down towards the stable floor; he had finished talking, and slipped into limbo mode. He could hear the young prince continuing to ask why, why, why, and with a flick of his ear had switched off the string of questions and was snoozing in his own time.

ELEVEN
A Pairing

The hound and his young bachelor companion had long since left the dam area and had been working the ridge lines linking half a dozen valleys. It was after one of their less successful forays had taken them down into man's domain that they came across a scent that caused both dogs to stop dead in their tracks and sample the droplets that hung from the cropped stubble of the freshly baled paddock.

As they inhaled the nectar from these droplets of light, their foreheads wrinkled in anticipation and their teeth began to chatter as their lips twitched uncontrollably.

The hound knew the scent well and with nose down was off and away; his brain engaged in one area only, to find the owner of the scent. He was closely followed by his companion, whose objectives were the same: the pursuit of desire.

The bitch had not mourned the loss of her litter for any appreciable time; life had returned to normal and her heat had come earlier than if she was suckling pups. She had let the world know of her availability, marking her travels with regularity, spotting the ground with droplets of desire, making sure that the weak and strong would be there to compete for her favours.

The bitch had taken to doing what she knew best, the raiding of domestic fowl. It was in her present condition that this form of hunting appeared favourable, as dogs that would normally give a warning growl, instead whimpered and strained against collar and chain in hopes of running with the scent. And so it was that one dog had pulled hard enough to snap a weak link in an old chain and set off in hot pursuit.

In an adjacent valley to the old man's farm, the bitch was enjoying the morning rays and showed no surprise when the farm dog with his broken chain still dangling from his collar came into the clearing. He came to an abrupt halt when he realised that the enchantment that he had so avidly been following was now directly in front of him. Now suddenly confronted with the possibility of succeeding in his quest he was put slightly off guard and stood as if glued to the spot, every fibre of his body looking as if it was connected to an electrical source, his ears standing taller, and every hair on his body looking as if it was alive and trying to dance the Light Fantastic.

The bitch paid this show little heed, what was foremost in her mind was the strength and ability of her suitors. She knew more would come, it would be the outcome of the battles that would follow that would determine the father of her pups. Until the next player in the game appeared she would keep this one hooked on a promise.

The two dogs had played in the sun, the bitch twisting and turning then running headlong with just enough speed to keep the farm dog one pace behind. Just when he thought he had managed to wear her down she would turn and show a set of snapping teeth.

His senses were dulled regarding anything else and as the hound burst upon the clearing and crashed hard into the kelpie, hitting the dog with his shoulder, causing the farm dog to roll over and over, leaving his throat unprotected. A few seconds later the hound's young travelling companion raced out of the tree line and much to his surprise and misfortune, ran straight into a victorious adversary.

The bitch had watched the demise of two mating prospects in less time than it takes to cover a scent and as the hound rolled in contempt on the inert bodies she raised herself up and urinated, captivating the hound's attention. The pair left the clearing as one, later to be joined many times in a union of strength and harmony.

TWELVE
Education Continues

The old man woke suddenly, registering that the log fire was now just a small ember and a thin line of smoke curling up towards the chimney.

He got up from his armchair, stretched and bent forward to pick up a log and hopefully rejuvenate the fire. He often awoke this way, not having made the comfort of his bed. His excuse being that if he was too comfy and relaxed, he might give in, or up, all depending how you looked at his logic - and possibly never wake again.

"Ho, hum and tickety boo," he said to himself and headed towards the percolator and his mandatory 'I'm still here', dark, strong coffee.

Across at the stables the stallion lifted his head and yawned… the yawn of a contented sleep that precedes the continuation of the last sentence spoken–however long ago that might have been.

The young occupant of the next door stable suddenly became aware that his mentor had started to talk of things long past.

"Have you had time to think of what has already been said?" and before the young colt could even think, he had started to continue the tale of the night before…

"On realising that the retreating hind quarter of the horse with no specific scent was paying him no attention whatsoever, the young colt lowered his head and began drinking again. And having sated his thirst, he watched the retreating horse, and without even thinking, he crossed the stream and followed. Being a herd spirit at heart, to follow without thinking gives a feeling of security."

In the next door stable his offspring had awoken to the continuation of last night's talk, and was trying to work out if he had missed anything.

"Heads down, the two horses were wending their way across the plains. The horse with no smell knew exactly what he was doing and where he was going, for this was a journey he had made many times before; the would-be Judas leading the unsuspecting seeker. With no apparent threat and no other visible company, the young colt had become, for the moment, the follower.

"They walked this way for many days, grazing and dallying amongst the different grasses ranging from clover to dry pick. They moved from water hole to water hole, enjoying life as bachelors in common, the only difference being one knew what he was, the other was just a young and impressionable young colt.

"As the pair moved on they occasionally came across small bands of mares and fillies with no stallion, just a lead mare who pushed or led the others wherever she wished. This meant nothing to the young colt who instantly pranced and paraded and becoming more familiar with the mares would lower his head and look as if he was snaking his way across the ground.

"The mares found it quite exciting to have so much attention, that they soon all fell into place next to and with the horse with seemingly no real purpose.

"Little did they know that he too had his own agenda and he knew exactly what he was doing and where he was going.

"The young colt knew no better and had absolutely no idea, except that he was now the proud leader and controller of at least forty-odd mares and probably thirty to thirty-five fillies of varying ages, from six months to eighteen months of age.

"With such a lack of experience of herd handling he was not really aware of how the horse with no scent had manipulated a few mares to do his bidding, as far as others straying was concerned, and just seemed to lead the herd and where he went they followed."

The young colt yawned loudly in his stable and the stallion in his was not impressed. All he said was,

"When you yawn, the movement of your jaw blocks out the sound; if you work out what you missed, we might continue, otherwise I have no more to say."

The old man sipped his second cup of coffee and turned the page on last weekend's newspaper: misreporting and keeping the public at large happy with sensationalism and ambiguous headlines. It gave him a considerable amount of amusement; journalism had long since lost the meaning of truth. He bent and put the paper in the fire lighting bin as he considered it was the most suitable place for a bad piece of journalism. Draining his coffee cup he contemplated briefly on its emptiness before heading back to the pot for a refill.

The old man drifted in and out of a state of doze, for some reason the days of yore kept re-enacting. His memories were a bit disjointed yet very poignant and at times vivid to the degree of making him start suddenly in the chair, only to slowly slump back into the memory or dream.

He had started perspiring only very slightly, yet he was damp, and a slight cool draught woke him, feeling completely chilled and a little confused. He was not at ease; coffee, maybe that was the answer, even though he had no great desire for it…

Something was wrong, his head was jumbled and his mind seemed quite a long way from the rest of him. His hands gripped the arms of his beloved chair and slowly, very slowly, he felt as if he was getting control. If only he knew what he was getting control of. He felt his chest, his heart was beating strongly and evenly; he checked his pulse on the meter thing that the district nurse had given him, and all was within the boundaries of safety, whatever they may be.

This meant only one thing - a disruption of his inner self; his peace and home-made tranquillity. Now came the hard part, the opening of the inner soul to see what had been disturbed. Things that were to lie dormant would have to be opened, scrutinised and then laid back to rest. This would become an agonising procedure, a tortuous journey into his past and the further back he may have to go, the more painful it could become.

He suddenly felt unbelievably tired and his breath was laboured. Life had over the years taken its toll and the last thing he needed was a trip backwards into all the dark corners that were just waiting to find his weakness; his Achilles heel, if you will.

Not now, not yet, he did not feel strong enough to embark on this trial of tribulation, the time was not right. Luckily he had not risen from his chair so the coffee he might have indulged in was not on the stove; there was nothing to simmer away and burn except his inner self and that could wait while his eyes closed and his breath slipped slowly from his mouth and slumber took over his tired frame.

Morning could never come too early, it was just that on this particular day he woke feeling tired, more inside his head than his body. Yet there seemed to be pains that he had always ignored as something that would go away - though as he lifted himself out of his chair he did not leave them behind. They travelled with him to the stove and nagged at his being; the pain was a constant annoyance - like the hum of a mosquito. He tried a stretch and that brought forth an exclamation through pinched lips.

He felt the cold tip of a muzzle rest itself in his hand and gently he fondled an ear, only to have it pushed away by another not quite so cold and rather dry nose. He looked down at the red dog and then let them both out, watching to see if the red dog ate some grass to get rid of whatever was bothering her.

She urinated and after surveying the activities in the yard, yawned and pottered back to the veranda. I will give her another hour, he thought to himself and then if her nose has heated any more, I had better check her out - a quick going over to see if there were any unduly sore spots.

The coffee smelt as good as ever and its fragrance beckoned him back to the stove. Pouring his cup and for some reason adding four heaped teaspoons of brown sugar, seldom heard of in his coffee agenda, he donned a jacket and scarf and headed for the veranda table maybe to listen to the farm waking, or maybe to turn on the radio and listen to the world's news of happy doom and gloom.

Resting one arm on the table to take the weight before lowering himself into the wooden chair suddenly caused a feeling he was not expecting - a twinge of pain that made him take a small intake of air; a bit like the red dog now lying at his feet, he would give himself a bit of a going over later.

The day was beginning …

"There is certainly no need to read the obituaries," he said out loud. Even though he never had the paper delivered he occasionally phoned a friend and said with a chuckle, "Go to the dead page and have a squizze, it would be good to see if I made it through the night," and they would both laugh…

He didn't bother with that bit of humour this morning because for all his pains, he knew that he was still here and he laughed again.

There were times when he thought back to parts of his life where things were best left to lie; events that could so easily become sadness capable of dragging him down into a mire. Many, he knew, would love to see this happen. Jealousy and lack of feelings of worth were sad things to observe in people.

Sometimes, when he and the stallion had entered their slow tired zone, where they both stood very quietly in the stable thinking very different thoughts yet bonded strongly; when closeness seemed to merge their spirits and they felt joined in a feeling of not so much sadness, more a longing, a camaraderie: never to allow any sadness in. A strange yet very intimate moment that could last for an hour or just a fraction of a second while two spirits aligned, gained strength and drifted slowly apart.

His mind was wandering now, his eyelids fluttering as he cruised off on a journey to who knows where; right now in a subconscious state all was so vivid and not always pleasant as life is not always as gentle as one would wish it to be.

As if in slow motion he watched the boot come towards his unprotected tummy. He knew without having to be told that it would hurt, and to top it all off it seemed to be happening with expert accuracy, just as the kick before had been. The assailant had come from nowhere, or rather from behind, and having a winter scarf wound twice around his neck it had made it easy for the much older and larger boy to swing him with ease and tie him up by the neck to a lamppost.

Max, of course, being his late father, would be angry - and not with the assailant, but with him for not being aware that there was someone behind him. His mother would be saddened that he had felt pain that she had not been able to avert, and also that the newly acquired even though second or probably third hand new coat was now soiled and sodden. Being England, the afternoon rain had made the dust into a semi- muddy substance, not thick brushable mud.

The boot collided with his young unclenched stomach muscles and he let out a half gasp, half moan, even though Maximillian had always said show no weakness, he was not there and this second boot attack really did hurt. Squinting through one eye so as not to show the tear that had been released he watched in amazement as the larger boy started to walk away laughing loudly and shouting out go back to where you came from, fucking refoe (refugee).

How did he know that he wasn't from here, what had given him away? He waited till the boy was out of sight and only then did he try to undo the knot in his scarf that held his neck tightly to the lamp post. Please don't let the street light come on till I've freed myself… it was 4.15pm and even though it was a very quiet little street it was Hampstead and people did walk their dogs towards Hampstead heath and also there were lots of little cottages on both sides of the road. It was the continuation of Flask Walk and led not only to the nearest pub, it also housed a little all-purpose shop where people would buy their packet of ten Weights or if they could afford it, Capstan or even a pack of twenty Senior Service, unfiltered of course.

The knot came loose and he was off fast and furious just as the street lights came on. He didn't realise quite what a mess he must have looked until he saw his mother's face as he called out and rushed up to her outside Sainsbury's on the Finchley Road. He had run himself ragged all the way down Fitzjohn's Avenue so that he could hopefully catch her and they could walk home together.

It was only then that his eyes welled up and the pain from the hard capped boot came into play. Such was life sometimes for an eight year old in the middle 50's. The face of the booted boy was indelibly printed on his memory bank and would be dealt with when he was a little older. The main object was to not let his mother see how hurt he really was, and thankfully his father was still on a ship somewhere heading home.

They arrived at their very small and meagre lodging; two rooms: a tiny kitchen-come eating place and one bedroom in a tenement type of block with shops underneath and rooms off the landings above toilets, but no bathrooms. It was diagonally across the street from Swiss Cottage underground station.

Bread and dripping and hot weak tea, Oh, the luxury of being at home with Mum.

His coat was already on a hook and as the little gas fire having been fed its sixpence started to give off heat, he watched as his mother got a damp cloth and began methodically wiping away the grime. He knew that a bit later on he would be asked what had happened, but for now there was peace, as his mother never rushed things, she always let them settle, before with what would appear to be interest (even though it was a mother's heart desperately crying out for her child's pain and wishing she could take it away) she would somehow extract the facts of the early evening's misfortunes. We had been through good and bad before, so she always tried to make the good outweigh the bad, and he loved her dearly for that and always told all, even though he would have liked to have kept some bits hidden.

The one thing that he did know was that if he made the whole incident a story, which would include his adventure on Hampstead Heath prior to his kicking, and the sighting of the big pike that moved from pond to pond by a series of underground waterways, it would become time for his bedtime story, which was never missed. At the moment they were in the middle of the Scarlet Pimpernel and he was totally enthralled with the dual identities of the hero, so he rambled with his woeful story as best he could, until his mother very quietly said,

"Get to the point, darling because the guillotine waits for no man and the crones are waiting to weave from the hair of the heads that fall."

That was when he knew he had been 'sprung', so they could get to France and see what was happening between the magical pages.

THIRTEEN
Touch and Go

His head jerked and he woke, not quite sure what he had been dreaming about. So, rubbing his ribs for no apparent reason he headed towards the inevitable coffee pot, thinking better check out that red dog to see where she is hurting.

Calling the red dog he headed for the veranda and with the best intentions started to run his hands over the dog to see if she winced at any of his touches.

There was a big lump just under the dog's armpit. All of his thoughts went into limbo: here was a problem that could easily become a disaster. He stood the dog up and pushed her as in play and she wagged her tail and took a step back towards him and her legs wobbled.

He felt the lump again and within seconds he had the tweezers pulled out from his Swiss Army knife and then began to sharpen the blade on the bush knife that he carried on his belt.

"It's OK my girl," he said reassuringly, and sliced around the offending lump.

She growled, pulling back her lips and revealing her canines. Her pale gums meant only one thing - the poison had started to travel around her body. She turned her head and stiffened; not that she would ever bite him, it was just to let him know that it hurt. He pushed the tweezers into her flesh on either side of the wound, wiping the blood away. Then he took the plunge and gripped the offending now visible head and with an extremely quick motion pulled and twisted hard and fast.

He then held the gorged item up to his glasses; yes, all the legs were there, wriggling and seeking the warm blood-giving area that it had been rudely removed from. The old man squeezed it till it popped and putting his fingers into Fox's mouth put the shell-back tick deep into her throat. Old wives' tale or not, as so many of the old boys did, he always fed the ticks back to the dogs to help their immunity. Hopefully the dingo in her would save her life.

To call the vet out and have him give her a shot would be useless, for a town dog maybe it would be the cure their owners wanted, but these dogs that lived and worked in the bush either lived or died. The shot that the vet would give would guarantee nothing except that it destroyed any immunity that the animal might have had. For this there was a hefty bill, and the knowledge that every time any form of tick, be it cattle or shell back, lodged itself into the dog's body, another shot would be necessary, as all self-produced immunity would now be lost.

All he could do now was to put her somewhere cool and not let her eat anything, slow her metabolism down to as low as possible - and hope. It would have been about three o' clock when the moaning started - he had put her in an old chair with winged sides, hoping that this would stop her from falling out. If she was about to leave this world then at the very least she had a form of comfort as it smelt of all the things she loved. Her head swung from side to side and the vomit spewed forth like a never ending projectile. He had never had a dog do this before and he had sat with quite a few of his four legged mates as they battled the inevitable when a shell back puts its poison into their bodies.

The sound was heart-breaking and as there was nothing he could do except clean her up, he felt a heaviness inside. Ten minutes later the same thing happened only this time her lips were drawn back and all her teeth were exposed as if she was fighting a demon - which of course she was. He filled a bag with ice and worked at keeping her cool. He did not take any notice of the time, it was irrelevant. The sound that emitted from her was like a cry from a heavy mist, my dear old friend, this hurts so much.

Her eyes were an opaque sort of colour. By the end of the second day he had not slept and the 22 rifle lay across his lap… just a bit more time, just a bit more… her pain was slowly eating into him and he knew that he really should put her out of her pain and misery. One shot whilst holding her head with his other hand and she would feel no more pain. He looked long and hard at her now waif-like body, for in the last two days she had lost all her weight and her coat was dull, and her odour, that normal dog-type smell had gone and all that was left was the smell of death.

It was then that she opened her eyes and she looked at him and he at her and he felt ashamed that he had the rifle on his lap for she knew what a gun was. He let his hand slowly run across her head and he held her ear. Patting the 22 he said very quietly,

"This was just in case an old carpet snake had wanted to wrap around you and squeeze you hard."

He pulled her ear and she squeaked, more from emotion than pain.

He got a large syringe from the horse first aid box and filled it with cold water and squirted it down her throat - maybe three or four times - and then sat on the edge of the chair, her head resting on his hand. He felt her tongue, rough and dry, slowly lick his palm and he knew, he just knew, she was over the worst and she had avoided death, or rather cheated Old Nick.

Much later when the sun was up he had headed for the stables lost in thought, thinking about the radical weight loss she had suffered. Bloody ticks, they are like some people he remembered from his past, once they were into you they just drained you from the inside out. Enough of this; Fox would live and there was a heap of stuff to catch up on.

FOURTEEN
Lessons Intensify

The stallion had been in his day yard while all this had been going on and happily munched his way through two bales of fresh, rich Lucerne hay - not the older shredded hay he would have put out if he hadn't been occupied with the dog.

The looseness of the stallion's bowels needed to be attended to right now. After finishing this, he had a quick look in the round yard and saw that the young colt had had a similar reaction to the very rich hay.

"Let's put you back in your stable while I clean up the round yard and then I'll get you together for today's work out."

It was going to be a tough morning and he winced as the pain in his back caught him unawares.

Unlike cow manure, chicken and horse manure can burn plants' roots unless it is broken down first. So the old man's breakdown process was to put the horse manure into forty-four-gallon drums, adding water and stirring every day. After a few weeks he could fill a watering can from the drums and water the vegetable garden with this rich feed.

He had swept and raked all the horse muck into three piles and went to get the small Kabota tractor. Then he had to shovel the muck into the tractor bucket and take it over to the back of the barn, where it would live for a few days before getting moved into the forty-four-gallon drums. The days and nights awake with the dog and now all this shovelling was making him tired and the veranda was looking more and more inviting by the minute. Only a couple more trips to the back of the barn and then maybe a cup of coffee before doing the hard feeds - and a general stroll round the place to make sure all was well.

The ringing of the telephone broke the tranquillity, and he grabbed it quickly,

"Speaking," he said quite tartly, and the voice at the other end just said "Happy birthday, old mate," and hung up.

One would have to be very brave or just plain stupid to stay on the line after a greeting like that. Birthdays were not recognised in this house, they had stopped when he was seventy-five and he often wished that they had stopped a long time before.

He found himself remembering remarks that people had made over the years, stuff that one would normally never take seriously–they were things people said and did in his business–in fact, any business–be it the horse business or the rag trade–wherever there are people; like animals in a pack there is always one who will be spiteful. The lead sledge dog in Call of the Wild, Spitz, who caused so much drama with the other dogs, until eventually they got fed up and turned on him. Just desserts they call it. This had to stop; he pushed the destructive thoughts out.

He was about to enter the round yard where in a few minutes the young colt would be back in the place with no corners. Life, as they say, often sends us a curly one - and the colt was about to have one placed fair and square upon him. He would, thought the old man, work it out and survive, as he was an intelligent little chap.

Just then, out of nowhere or so it would seem, the red dog hit him hard behind his right leg, as she tried to catch up to him at a wobble. It would not be long before her hindquarters were back to normal but right now she was a bit all over the place with control of the back legs not quite as it should be. The old man smiled at this attempt to keep up with him - she was definitely a fighter.

He had never forgotten the day when he had been cutting back an area of lantana and two days later had felt an annoying itch and slight pain in the back of his head. That was where the little bugger had latched on and now came the painful yet very necessary removal of the tick before it made him sick. It's not easy when you have to work with two mirrors and a pair of tweezers. He put a little iodine on its backend before he started to dig it out. He knew that the next time he was cutting back lantana (an herbaceous weed) he would wear a skull cap of some description, and check his whole body once he was in the shower.

Now that he had hold of the small lead rope that hung off the colt's halter and was headed for the round yard, another day in the colt's education was about to begin. They entered the round yard and before the colt realised it there was a leather strap around his chest that was slowly being tightened one notch at a time. He flinched just a little and tried to move away from the old man, but that didn't work; and as the man gently scratched behind his ear, the colt leaned into his new friend and bent his head to one side, his nose twitching just enough to put a smile on the old man's face.

He was slowly getting a closer relationship with the young colt and that was always a good feeling. He had locked the red dog out of the yard, much to her disgust, but he really didn't need her wobbling around, for her safety as much as his own.

The wall-eyed bitch was by his heel watching as usual just in case she was needed. Her old friend was standing in the middle of the round yard with a long rope now attached to the colt's head collar. Very quietly he had clipped it on to the round brass ring and now he was just waiting for the first move that might be made in relation to the girth strap now firmly attached around the young colt's body.

To say the colt was a little confused was an understatement, but that would soon pass; after he had tried to nip the leather and given a half-hearted buck he would soon lose interest in the leather strap and start to wonder about the long piece of rope attached to his head collar. He had become used to the small piece of leather that was attached to the head collar from day one, as it only hung down about a foot and that was what the old man got hold of every time he came near him. But this was much longer and made him feel that he was not exactly free… he felt that he was somehow restrained and could be pulled up at any given moment.

The old man just stood in the middle of the round yard and rolled a cigarette, and the colt heard the scratch and inevitable flame, as the man lit the rolled piece of paper that protruded from his lips. The small plume of smoke lifted gently upward and disappeared into the air; he could smell something strange - it was neither pleasant nor unpleasant; it was a smell he had come to associate with the man, it was on his clothes and seemed to be a part of him. So many things to take in, so many intrusions, that he must remember to ask the stallion about.

The leather strap that laid across his back was no longer of any great interest; the rope hanging loosely from his head collar down into saw dust and then all the way to the man was now his main concern as he tried picking it up and chewing it. He shook it; tossing his head up in the air. It did not fight back, it didn't hurt him, but it didn't go away, either. It was still there, just hanging - just another thing that he had to come to terms with.

The round yard had a canopy over it so that it could be used in all weathers. Hanging down from the middle cross beam was a piece of rope with a hook on it. The old man had attached the rope to the hook, which was on a swivel and had left the yard quietly and without fuss. The colt found himself alone except that everywhere that he went the rope went too. He was never without it being right there with him all the time. He tried cantering round and round and then galloping; the rope was still with him.

There was no pressure, but also no escape, alone with a rope in a place with no corners. What was he to do next? What was there to do except just accept the situation and potter about every now and then, trotting or cantering or just walking; there was nothing else he could do. Yet he wasn't caged, he had freedom, it was just that he really could not go anywhere; a strange feeling indeed. So he stood very still and waited to see what would happen next.

The old man went over to the stallion and talked long and slow; every now and then the stallion would shake his head as if he understood what was being said. It was actually his response to an annoying fly that would not go away. The conversation over, the old man headed for the veranda, the wall-eyed dog close by his heel.

The red dog, with great determination, even though she had a sideways lean to her made a valiant effort to be as close to man and dog as she possibly could. The steps up to the veranda were an obstacle she would have to work out when she got there, such was the determination to be close to her friend. There is nothing in this world like the loyalty of a four-legged companion.

Jock of the Bush Veldt about the terrier who fought many a battle with baboon, man, and mysterious animals that he came across, or *The Call of the Wild*, about the dog stolen from its loving home only to be transported and sold as a fighting dog in the far North, are tales that serve to illustrate the fierce bond that can be developed between man and dog.

By the time that Fox had made her way up the steps the old man had got his coffee and was seated at the table. She wobbled over to him and he gently tugged her ear as she slumped down next to his chair. The wall-eyed dog gave her one of her welcoming growls.

The colt was in the round yard, head down, in a sleepy sort of trance, the rope just lying on the ground and then up to the hook in the middle of the canopy. The stallion was in a similar position, his head lolling over the stable door, one hind leg cocked and resting on the point of his toe.

Another day in paradise, as the saying goes; if only they had all known what was brewing on the other side of the mountain range that separated them from the neighbouring valley.

FIFTEEN
Fire

The UTE sped across the dirt at a speed that was more than just frightening; the lad at the steering wheel was following the large 'roo without any regard for safety at all; his two mates egging him on, calling him every name under the sun for not getting closer, till the one on the passenger side flicked his cigarette out of the window, grabbed the 22 from his mate's lap and took a hurried shot at the bounding buck - missing - and blasted off a second shot with even less accuracy.

"Give it up, mate," the lad in the middle said, "let's get to the hotel and have a beer, this is a joke - you couldn't hit a barn door at twenty paces."

Testosterone was at its height and if it hadn't been for the cramped conditions in the UTE, punches would have been thrown. The driver got back on the main track and headed out of the valley, and by the time they got to the hotel it would all be a big joke and they would laugh their way through five or six schooners, telling anyone who wished to hear what a great chase they had been in with a big daddy 'roo. And so the evening would go on till they decided to call it a night and try to beat the coppers home, full of grog and bad manners.

The cigarette end had landed on dry grass turned brown by the sun over the last few weeks and it wasn't long before it had started to smoulder, slowly at first, until a gust of wind stirred the embers into a tiny flame. It was not long before that flame had transformed into a small fire, fanned by a breeze that had come out of nowhere.

The fire started to branch out and take hold of twigs and small pieces of dead wood, with dried grasses giving it fuel; it flared up, running along the ground, ever eager to consume as much as it could. Within 15 minutes the small ember from the end of the missile flicked out of the UTE by a lad who should have known better had turned into what would become one of the first big fires of the dry season. It had taken hold and would soon race along the valley floor and onto the side of the hillside. Once catching hold of the dry shrubs at the base of the hillside and the dry timber on the lowland forest floor, the flames would soon catch the dry gum leaves, popping and spraying sparks all around.

The birds had long left the branches and the small mammals were in flight, with the fire close on their heels. Echidnas, mice and voles stood no chance and the 'roo's, wallaby's, deer and wild pigs were bounding up the hills at a rate of knots.

On the valley floor cattle were on the move; they had come across the first set of barbed wire fences and had milled around until one of the more forceful steers had jumped the five-stranded fence. The rest had followed, some getting tangled up in the barbs which tore at their legs, causing large gashes, some clean through to the bone. If they didn't manage to free themselves they became terribly entangled and the chances of escaping were nigh on impossible and would only be achieved by the farmer's hand using heavy duty wire cutters. This was never an easy job as the terrified beast would kick and struggle, making it not only difficult but incredibly dangerous. Eventually the wire was pushed down onto the ground by the sheer mass of cattle, still leaving a dangerous obstacle that grabbed at their hocks, tripping them over and over again.

Both sides of the valley had become a war zone as far as the bush fire brigade would be concerned - and as yet they didn't know anything was amiss. The plume of smoke had started to rise into the night sky and all that anyone would see would be a reddish glow through a mist. It would be the smell of burning timber that would ring alarm bells and then it would be all on: phones would start to ring and the bush fire brigade would drag out the old Blitz; if there was a track, then no mountain would stop her, she would just grind away, engine roaring, as the gears came down to first as the hill got steeper and she climbed up into the fire zone.

How they would attack this particular fire was yet to be seen; the inevitable was at hand: complete destruction of a beautiful hillside that would in time grow back, but some of the big blue and grey gums would be lost forever. All this brought on by one stupid boy and a fag end; he would never admit his folly and it probably wouldn't occur to him or his sleeping drunk mates that they had anything to do with the disaster. Their only comment would probably be, "Bet that old 'roo got his arse singed," as they downed another schooner.

The old 'roo, like many others, had died long before the flames had reached him. They had run ahead of the fire, terrified by the crackling and the heat along the valley floor, all the way to the base of the cliff at the end. Whilst wild dogs could climb the cliff face and narrow precarious tracks, the 'roo's could not. By this time there was quite a mob of old boys, young males, does and joeys in and out of their mothers' pouches, all tired and with nowhere to go.

They had milled around in confusion and some had started back along the valley where they were confronted by a dense curtain of smoke that was hard on the lungs, burning as they gasped for breath. Many didn't make their frantic dash for freedom as they succumbed to the smoke. Some who had got higher up the hill in front of the main body of flame carried large patches of singe marks; others fractionally behind the leaders were covered in hot ash, their fur still smoking.

The once tall trees were now standing like glowing beacons in the dark, their sap boiling and spraying out red hot sparks, keeping the fire alive and even more destructive.

The horses at the home farm were uneasy and the dogs were restless. The old man woke up in his chair and knew instantly that something was amiss; and as he opened the door onto the veranda he was confronted by that awful glow high in the sky that meant only one thing; a bush fire and a big bush fire at that. He moved back into the room and picked up the phone, the line gave the busy tone and he hoped the wires weren't down.

He tried again and this time it was answered,

"Bush fire brigade, what's your position?" said the voice on the other end. With his distinctive voice there was no doubt who it was,

"It's me," he said.

"Christ, are you all right mate? We've just been told it's nearly at the top of the mountain and could drop down into your place real soon. Better get the bad bit over with, eh… the old school house has already gone, mate. We're really sorry, it's all, well, you can imagine what it's like over there. The fire ran along the river and burnt everything. It's all gone, mate."

The old man stood there for a second and seemed to shrink as he took in the news about his beloved school house down on the river flats. His shoulders had sagged, then as if he had been filled with an unknown power, he pulled them up and found himself saying into the mouthpiece,

"It's all just a big glow at the moment, mate, it hasn't come over the top yet," his hand shaking just a little.

"Right mate, don't go anywhere, we will get back to you in about ten minutes."

"OK," said the old man, putting down the phone and heading for the stove to get the coffee heating up.

Then he opened the door to the veranda, walked to the handrail and holding it very tightly took in the full extent of the situation.

"Gone," he thought, the old school house burnt to the ground, a part of history; not just his, but of all the families that had cut timber. 'Feather legs' was the name given to the members of the church that had ridden over the mountain every week on a perilous track to give religious instruction and support to all the local children from the surrounding farms in the school building.

And then all of a sudden all hell broke loose in his head - he had decided not to put the big Percheron cross Shire mare back in foal and instead taken her to the old hill paddock and thrown in two other mares in with her for company. None of them had coupled with the stallion so they could just have a gentle year and not have to carry a foal until the following season. What about the three of them, how would they be fairing during this awful event?

He would not be able to check on them until the fire had passed and even then not until the ground had cooled down enough for the stallion to walk on. He hated to wait but he had no choice, so he put the worry away in a space that wouldn't cloud what had to be done now, which was to secure his farm and his stock. The phone jangled and he made his way back inside,

"We are on our way over to make a fire brake," was the crackled message - and that was it, the line went dead.

"Well, that's the phone out, better get to work and soak as many outbuildings as I can, just in case."

He headed out to the connecting point that had to be reset to make all the hoses line up to the sprinklers that sat on top of the stables, the barns and round yard. The sprinklers would soak the buildings thoroughly. In a situation like this the timber slabs would have to be wet enough to withstand an enormous amount of heat otherwise the water would boil and evaporate quicker than the blink of an eye. He would have to water the chook shed manually as it was a slightly newer addition. Luckily he had pumped water up from the river only a few days ago and all the water tanks were full. As an added precaution, he started the big pump up and sucked up more water to keep the tanks filling as they pumped water to all the sprinklers.

His house had a separate system and he went to attend to that and get the four sprinklers spraying out across the tin roof and with downpipes blocked it cascaded over the guttering and soaked the slab walls. He had set all of this up much to the dismay of his friends and visitors who could not understand the relevance of his thinking: the once in a lifetime threat. Here it was and he just hoped that his handiwork was enough to keep this fire at bay.

Now back down to the barn, as it was filled with dry bales of hay, oats and Lucerne. To keep the outside wet and the contents inside dry was not an easy task. The barn held six loose boxes which he had to get the mares from the home paddock into; they had to come in just to be on the safe side. There might only be four of his herd left, but in panic mode it would be like trying to stop a locomotive that was out of control.

He looked up at the mountain and there it was in all its frightening glory, the fire had breasted the top and was starting to make its way down the hill, the flames licking hungrily at anything in their way.

His breathing seemed to be slowing him down, and in the back of his mind he knew that after ten years of not smoking because of the valves that were in his left lung and the weakness in his right, that he should never have started to smoke again. His logic had been that a few ‘roll your own’ and half a cigar in the evening, if not inhaled, would not hurt. He was, let’s face it, at that end of his life and he did enjoy it so much.

Unfortunately, it was now that he felt it, mainly because he had to move faster than his normal stroll and his chest started to burn with pain as he gasped and strained to breathe.

Slow down my son, he said to himself - less haste more speed - you will get it all done if you just stay cool and groovy. He would have laughed at his logic if his breath had been easier to control.

He headed for the veranda. There was a supply of oxygen inside the house, unused for a long time, but he was starting to realise that without it all could be lost. He slowed right down and took long deep breaths through his nose and tried to control his heart rate and slow everything down. Bugger getting old and bugger all the people that used to tell him how sick he was, for he was sure that their bad energy had made him worse.

But now the important objective was get to the all-important oxy. Deep down, he knew he would be fine, it was just a question of no panic, go at the pace that suited the occasion… it was not easy yet it was achievable and if anyone could do it he could. And he would, so head down and his determination set, he made it to the steps.

The rest would be as it would be, and what came into his mind was the story of his mate he had sailed with on many occasions, who had fallen over board from the good ship Truesan, a forty-foot ketch. He watched as the mainsail became a cross on the horizon and then suddenly reappeared and came back towards him. He never panicked till the sail boat was twenty or so feet away and only then did his heart race at the thought of sharks, for up until then it was just an adventure but with the yacht so close it was a feeling of 'Not now, please, not now'. And that is how the old man felt as he started on the first step of the veranda, grasped the hand rail and took one step at a time.

Later, in the stables, sounds and vibrations could be heard and felt by the stallion and colt; the old man had put on deep soulful music at an even louder volume than usual, mainly to drown out the sound of the generator that was now thumping away. Thc clcctricity pylons had bccn a casualty of the fire, buckling under the intense heat and releasing the wires to add more sparks to the inferno.

The stallion took a deep breath; he coughed slightly as the air now carried a faint trace of burning timber that irritated his sensitive lungs. This was not a good sign and he was just a little agitated by its presence. No matter, he was in his stable and his friend was at hand, so he considered that he was comparatively safe for the time being at least.

Outside the first of three four wheel drives sped into the yard at the front of the house and the bright yellow uniforms spilt out even before the Toyota had come to a halt. The old man was sitting at the table on the veranda; the men came up the steps two at a time, the first one up noticed the portable oxygen bottle leaning against the balustrade.

"Are you alright, mate? Do you want us to get you out of here and up to the hospital?"

It was only a small facility but carried everything that a bush emergency might need.

"No, no, I am just fine," he said, taking the cannula off his nose. "Just getting a boost of the old oxygen, no big deal. Now grab some cold water out of the bar fridge and tell me what the situation is like around the place. Is every one safe? Any other buildings other than the old school burnt out? Or do you need to bring people here?"

"So far, so good," was the reply, "A few sheds have gone, but apart from that, everyone seems safe. You were the main worry out here on your own but you seem to have it under control."

He winked as the old man asked about the fire breaks,

"Didn't work, mate, she bloody jumped the tracks and kept on going. We have five more trucks turned up and we are about to start cutting the brush out of the bottom of that hill and then we can soak it all from the river, if you are ok about us driving over that far pasture."

"Not a problem, I got the mares in first thing so you can just leave the gates open and go for it. Anything you need me to do?" he asked wistfully.

"Yes mate, there is, if you wouldn't mind,"

"Just ask," he said. "Keep the coffee on and make up some silverside sandwiches, if that's ok."

"All cool, buddy, not a problem."

"Oh, and one more thing,"

"Name it," he said.

"Just don't die on us, ok?" He slapped the old man on the back and laughed as he jumped down the steps, "As if you would, hey? Outlive us all, you old bastard, that you will."

And he climbed into the tojo and with a grinding of gears they set out in four-wheel drive to attack the tree line before the fire got to it.

Well, the old man mused to himself, if they stop the fire what they cut down will be next year's fire wood, that's one job I won't have to tackle! And he coughed into a handkerchief and noticed a faint red streak in his phlegm.

"Bugger," he said and headed for the stove and a hot cup of coffee, putting the offending tissue into the fire box.

It was probably just a scratch causing a tiny bleed, he mused, no need to be dramatic. That was how he approached these small setbacks these days; so much better than always looking at the negative.

So many of what he considered lucky people did. The easier they had their lives the harder they made them out to be. They didn't work, they just did everything for everybody else - only the people in question didn't always want what the person was offering. It seemed that saying how much they did justified the fact that they went round in circles to somehow cover up their guilt for something only they knew.

Such is life in the western world, how jolly good did that coffee smell, it seemed to be even more intoxicating than usual… the joys of simplicity, and then he chuckled, as the fire raged across the mountain. He meant no disrespect to the many animals that were suffering, it was just that the fire was indeed raging and he was enjoying his coffee; that was just how it was. So he sat on the veranda watching the bush fire brigade working their chain saws and keeping his eyes on the spray from the sprinklers as it fell on the outbuilding's roof lines, he hoped that his friends in their outlying properties were OK.

He was there if needed and there was food and tea and coffee and a cold beer for any who needed a little solace. And there could be a few of them, including the over-heated and raggedy bush fire boys who by now were covered in sweat and sawdust and desperately trying to breathe in the smoke-filled tree line.

SIXTEEN
A Cautionary Tale

The stallion had rested for a while and clearing his throat, he seemed to gather his thoughts and returned to the story of the horse with no scent and the young colt with his new-found herd of mares.

"It was nearly too late by the time that the colt realised that he could be walking into a trap laid by man. For the horse with no scent had had kept pushing the mares in a certain direction, which was the way it had been for many years now. He seemed to meander slowly among the mares and the young colt, who was enjoying the dalliances that he was having with the mares.

"The track he was taking was well trodden and had been the demise of many a young colt in their youthful exuberance - only to end up in a man-made yard. And then thrown to the ground, stretched out and cruelly having their stallion-hood cut away. And if they survived the ordeal they would stand for hours on end suffering massive swelling and bruising to their wound. Their fate was to be determined at a later date - either to be broken to the saddle and used as a beast of burden, or sent away to be used for dog food - or just left to die, if their suffering meant they could no longer walk.

"Only just in time did the colt realise that all was not well and with a snort and a small prance he was off up the slip path that led away from the closed off valley and up the mountain to freedom and a new life. There he would find mares of his own, without a Judas to take him where no young colt should go.

"The horse with no scent was always rewarded for his work with a stay in a warm stable for a few days, with good hard food, fresh clear water and lush hay to drool over until he was released once again. He would begin his trek again on the far side of the hill, finding more mares and maybe a young colt in the same narrowing valley. This would give the men another batch of new horses to sell on, for work under the saddle, or as pack animals or as food."

At the end of the tale, there was a long silence and then the stallion said,

"Do you understand what I've told you?"

The young colt was confused but didn't wish to admit his failure to grasp the whole meaning of the tale and so answered simply, "Yes".

Silence once again reigned; the stallion slept with a vague sense of foreboding triggered by the smell of smoke in the air, and the young colt had a confused and restless time trying to fathom out the story. In time, and with a few more clues, he would unravel the message.

Now he collected his thoughts, trying to work out the new smell that irritated his nostrils and was unpleasant to taste, and induced a feeling that he would later realise was fear.

SEVENTEEN
The Aftermath

Ollie the owl and his new found mate were perched on an upright plank of wood; behind him three young owls were looking out at the fire in the distance and wondering what it was all about as none of them, not even Ollie, had ever been in a bush fire before - let alone a fire of this density - and sitting still seemed the most sensible thing to do.

The bookends were curled up on the back of the sofa at the farm, totally ignoring what was going on outside, and the dogs were at their master's feet waiting to see what he would do next.

The wild dog pack had reached their goal, of finding relative safety from the fire and were relaxing as best they could in the circumstances. Some of the older dogs stretched out resting and the younger ones were more active, even though very tired after their long climb to their safe vantage point. The smell of charred bodies and smoke filled the air. They were at the beginning of the high part of the forest and if luck held, the flames would not reach this far up and they would be safe for the time being.

Leaning against the veranda railing watching the flames and the tiny figures of the bush fire brigade boys starting and restarting their chain saws, the old man could also see other figures way in front aiming the long hoses that ran out from the Blitz. There were also two other far more modern vehicles pumping water out of the large dam at the bottom of the slope at the start of the fire break. The break had to be soaked to such a degree that as the flames hit it the water didn't start to boil and evaporate.

Standing watching, the old man started to reminisce and drift into times gone by; as his subconscious roamed in the past he became almost oblivious to the heat and the fire. If he were a horse or a dog he would have shook his head to clear his thoughts but he just came to his senses, every thought that was trying to come back and invade his space was sent back to a 'look at later' place. Strange that some things from a long way back were suddenly coming to the fore as if they needed to be addressed or remembered with clarity before… before what?

He realised it was time to pay the stables a visit, tidy up a bit and make a fuss of the two lads and try to take their minds off the smoke that was now filtering into every nook and cranny it could find. He wanted to make sure that the slab walls were retaining the water that was streaming over them from the roof sprinklers. He had better check the pump fuel as well, a bit like his cars, he hated them running dry, dragging all the crap into the valves and injectors. Just one of the old man's foibles, of which it could be said there were many.

So with a slight sigh he moved slowly onto the first step and down into the yard below, the two dogs close on his heels.

All these thoughts of the past gave his present some credence. He had a future, too, how long a one was of no importance, as he had learnt over the years that between one's own anatomical short falls, there was always the horse that unseated you; the truck that didn't miss you, and some megalomaniac in a far off land that had just decided to blow everything to buggery, as the saying goes.

Still, no excuse to drag one's feet along like some old fart in a wind storm - stand up straight and walk tall. And he put a spring in his step and the dogs wagged their tails. The old boy was on the move and everything was tickety-boo.

The stallion heard him coming from across the yard and blew through his nose and nickered a greeting. The young colt tried to copy him and was surprised at the fact that he, too, had said hello. Ah, well, why not, nobody else around to talk to, so he did it again, ears pricked forward as he leaned against his stable door.

"Well, well, well, here's a turn up for the book. I didn't expect him to come to terms with accepting me quite so quickly; life is full of surprises."

And once again the old man felt his mind wandering to another time and place, but he nipped it in the bud very damn fast, as the last thing you need is your brain out on a different limb when dealing with another independent being. A horse, like a woman, can spot a weakness a mile away and you are just asking to get kicked - and ain't that the truth.

He totally ignored the colt and went straight to the stallion's stable. Off with the old, on with the new - never. In his book, loyalty was first and foremost; you might not have had contact with the horse, dog, or person for years, but the original ground rules are set in concrete and are never, ever forgotten. He had learnt that by years of experience. He had seen too many people switch and swerve and when the real crunch came and the friend was needed they were not there. So, the rule was, stallion first, colt later. Anyway, it would irk the young fellow to think he was being ignored; then again the stallion would explain it all to him during their private time together.

He glanced outside and down the paddock, just making out the figures through the smoke; they were still frantically getting their fire break set. He would have been with them a few years ago, fighting as hard as they were, if only his lungs and one or two other small bits of him had not started to degenerate. He cursed low and under his breath, for the stallion knew his every move and most of his feelings.

The stallion was a little edgy; the smells from the fire were not attractive to his sensitive nose and he was thinking of his mares and of his own survival. Not that the old man had not thought of the big mare and the two others in the Fairy Wood on the other side of the river from the burnt out school house, already a sadness that would never go away….

There had been many such losses during his lifetime. As with everyone, nobody goes unscathed. His rule of thumb was: if you are on this earth then life was not meant to be easy; fun, scary and sometimes heart-breaking, but never, ever, easy.

The stallion shook his head and he scratched him under the chin. He could feel the tension in the horse, and he tried very hard to take the worry out of his hands so that all that the stallion felt was his old friend right there, as if nothing was wrong. If it worked, great - if not - well, you can't fool them all the time. Just be aware that because the horse was distracted there was always the possibility of a 'cow kick' or even a quick nip or even a bite; not intended for him, exactly, just the tension in the animal coming to the fore. So, keep your wits about you, old boy, he means you no harm, it just comes down to fear of the unknown and survival.

He went all over the stallion's back, massaging gently, yet with enough pressure to make the horse's top lip twitch, and he screwed his neck around at a ridiculous angle looking to be scratched. It was at these times that he had to be very aware as the old horse had been known to nip very hard out of sheer pleasure - unfortunately not yours.

His eyes rolled in his head and his back twitched and rippled in his own form of ecstasy.

"Well, old mate, that is enough for now, I reckon," and with that he placed a light day rug on the horse as the heat from the fires meant that a night rug wasn't needed.

This light cover would give some protection from the insects that had been gathering in the safety of the stable. And before the stallion realised it, the old man was out and had closed both the bottom and top door of his stable.

"Now for the young colt," the old man was in his stable very quickly but calmly and had attached the lead rope to the colt's halter and then clipped it onto a ring quite high up on the side of the stable wall.

All this did was to stretch the young horse's head and neck out and upward so that he did not have the balance to either buck or kick as the old man rearranged his bedding. This was a small safety precaution that he considered necessary with these extreme conditions. A jittery young colt is not a good thing to be caught in tight conditions with, especially one who was just learning his manners; better safe than sorry.

Anyway, the young horse was now intent on nibbling the end of the rope and his attention was away from the man in his stable. Suddenly his ears pricked up and one of the dogs gave a small warning growl - nothing to be alarmed at - he would check it out as soon as he had put a day rug on the young fellow. No sooner thought than done, and once again as quickly as he came in he had unclipped the rope and was out of the doors, locking both top and bottom securely. If by chance the fire did manage to get up to the farm he knew that the guinea fowl would set up an amazingly loud clatter - not always what you want to hear on a quiet moonlit night, yet still a great warning system against fire, foxes, and unwelcome shadows.

As he approached the veranda it became obvious why the dog had given her warning. There were six of the fire brigade on the veranda, looking much the worse for wear.

"Helped ourselves to a coldie, mate, knew you wouldn't mind,"

"Not a problem," he said. "Get it down you and grab another, quick as you can - you must be hot as hell."

"Mate, I tell you we might just have got it beat. There's another crew down there now and if the fire doesn't jump you have about four years of firewood all stacked up in piles. You'll just have to make them log size."

"Jesus, boys, that's a bit slack, the least you could have done was cut them up for me, slack buggers that you are."

They all laughed and one of the older members of the brigade said,

"I'll tell you what, old mate, that dam has got to be one of the best around, I can remember swimming in her when I was a nipper; got flogged for it too. Never did get to the bottom of her - she's well deep. Always a lot of catfish and crays I seem to remember."

"Still are," the old man said, "Did you know that the young catfish attach themselves to the ducks' feet and when the duck lands in a new dam they just drop off. That's how they get into brand new dams."

There was silence for a minute then,

"Yeah, right mate, they use the ducks as taxis, is what you're saying."

"Oh, and of course I stock her up with bass every year; fingerlings, that's a great fighting fish: you can spin for them or take them off the bottom, all depending on what they're eating at the time. Grubs, worms, crickets catch a few and then again I have caught a lot with a little mouse on a hook as well."

"Well mate, we pumped and pumped and the water mark hasn't even dropped; those bloody springs are a beaut."

"Reckon they are, buddy, reckon they are, I used to swim the horses in her up until two years ago. Don't now, just in case I come a cropper, I don't think I would make the swim to the bank."

"Shit, mate, don't go drowning on us, who would stock up your beer fridge?"

More laughter then another round of 4X was in their hands and soon up to lips that hardly hit the rim before the cold liquid was gushing down parched throats.

"You know old mate, I wouldn't be surprised if there was a big damp old mist come in tonight. It sort of has that feel to it."

"And what feel is that, exactly?" said one of the younger members of the brigade.

"One that you may never live to find out, young fella, if watching you trip over everything that lay on the ground was anything to go by."

"You could be right, you know, look at the bookends, they don't give a damn about fires and they are well wedged inside. They don't mind the wet but they hate heavy mist, it clings to their fur," said the old man.

"If you're right that mist will dampen down a bit… the big gums that are alive with fire inside are the worry, they will smoulder for weeks. Oh, by the way, any sign of that dog pack, the bitch is back you know, and running with one of the Prescott boys pigging dogs. Shit, she is a canny dog that one."

"Nope, we didn't see any sign but hey, let's face it, there isn't much about that's not dead or dying. It's hit the wildlife hard on this side of the range. Only good thing I suppose is the snakes have been given a hurry-up. Lots of brown bastards around this year, and I hate them."

"Same here," said the old man, remembering one memorable journey home with his heel on the brown snake's head stuck between his RM Williams boots and the stirrup iron.

That had been a day and a half - the big old brown had raised himself up three feet into the air and come at the stallion from the side, aiming for the old man's leg. He had misjudged his strike and clamped onto the stirrup iron; the old man had jammed his heel down on the snake's head, and with the tail thrashing about like a wind sock in a gale the stallion was not impressed. Five miles they travelled like that, and some ride it was too. The problem was, on reaching the farm, what to do with the snake who was very much alive, and very pissed off at having its head half crushed. It was on the right hand side of the horse, which made dismounting just a little hazardous. Luckily, there was an old mate in the yard come to scrounge some farrier gear and all he could say to him was 'cut its bloody head off and don't bloody well hit my leg.' The head of a black or brown snake can still inject poison even when it is not connected to its body. The fangs are still active and the poison still flows.

Snakes and scorpions have the same agenda - if it's in the way, destroy it. The only difference between them is that if the scorpion is so threatened that it can see no retreat, it stings itself to avoid losing to an aggressor, or even to a ring of fire; maybe it just cannot bear to be seen as a loser.

Sometimes the female scorpion will kill the male following mating, in a fight for supremacy. It is not just survival that drives the human race it is also the battle for supremacy - the winning at all costs syndrome. This drive is to find the weakness in your opponent at any cost.

Just watch the Jodhpur clad young lady who carries the whip with a seemingly all-powerful horse. A prime example is in the Arab show-ring where even some of the 'most successful' have been known to bring a beautiful creature to its knees in a state of mental or physical distress just by lifting an arm, or the whip, to induce a state of fear.

But the underdog can turn, too: the pony in India that says to itself 'what is the point, it is always going to hurt so let's stop it now' and turns and viciously attacks its handler. Or the sledge dog that sees an opening and attacks the leader, or another bullying dog that has made its life a misery.

And so it happens in the human world, the age old way of conquering by dominance that in many cases causes violence and tragedy. And they try to dominate the animal kingdom with knowledge that does not work; to be the supreme master and to rule without compassion.

The drive for supremacy leads some people to get a buzz out of what they consider is winning, only to find that they end up lonely and sad; left only with their own guilt and a sense of loss that they can't quite understand.

And so endeth the most important lesson: you get more with honey than with vinegar; the old man loved that line more than any other.

EIGHTEEN
Loss

Thank the earth for the stallion and the silly peacock and thank the heavens for the rain; the old man snapped out of his dreaming ramblings. He registered the pitter-patter on his tin roof - that could only mean one thing. The boys had been right, there had been a feeling of moisture in the air and here it was in the pattering droplets of water; if it continued, then good, steady rain might be here by the morning and life would regain a semblance of normality. He could feel his head clearing as the drops got bigger and the sound became a steady drumbeat on the roof. No thunder, no wind, just a steady, beautiful, rhythmical melody.

In the stables the temperature had dropped by a degree and the two horses felt no more pressure from the intense heat and the invasive smoke.

The frogs in the dam started to call out to one another in their never-ending quest to propagate with as many willing frogs as possible while the time was right. The rain had arrived and was here for a few days at least. There would be frog spawn on the water surfaces tomorrow, be it in the dam or in puddles; within days there would be tadpoles everywhere.

The nitrogen that the fire's carnage had left behind in the form of ashes would be pushed deep into the soil and rejuvenation would start; green shoots would begin to appear. The slow burning, inner-lit logs would start to dim, their red hot sap lines slowly being extinguished and start to smoke as the heat was relinquished to the cooling rain. The regeneration process would start again, but the only problem was that each time this happened it took longer and there were less births and more creatures became closer to becoming endangered, and that of course, brought us back to man.

With his thoughts drawn to the destruction around, the old man could feel himself getting low again, which would never do, so the remedy was coffee and some gentle music. Blues was the first thought that came to mind and then for no rhyme or reason, he put on Sibelius, very softly, and in unison with the rain on the roof his mind wandered onto calmer thoughts.

The bookends started purring as his hand gently ran over their fur and they both slightly raised their back ends so as not to miss one caress that might linger at the base of their tails. This was a spot that in most animals had a great calming effect that was almost euphoric.

Life was coming back to level ground and the pain that had started to encroach on his thoughts started to dull. He placed his coffee cup on the small round table next to his chair. A small smile crossed his face and his hand dropped onto the red dog's head and she yawned peacefully. The glow from the fire gave a harmonious effect to his world and his eyelids started to come together as peace reigned.

He was awoken by a noise that did not fit in with the rain or the bookends purring. It was a thump and then a muffled whistle. He pulled himself upright and went to the door onto the veranda. Hitting the light switch he looked out and sitting on the floor was a very disgruntled looking Ollie. He had just decided that it would be more comfortable in his original home and not thinking that the old man would have closed the window had glided into the glass and crumpled onto the veranda floor. His head was tilted back and his big mouth was wide open. A frogmouth owl has a large and deep throat.

When he had first found the owl, years back, sitting on the side of one of the steep tracks up the mountain, he was a few weeks old and had obviously fallen out of his parents' hole in one of the trees, or been pushed out by an intruder such as a cuckoo. And there he was with his new feathers and a gaping mouth, unfazed by his fall and just waiting to be fed. The old man thought he was just like Oliver Twist asking for more, and thus the name Ollie Beak.

He put his hand down and over Ollie's back, picking him up and carrying him inside. He put him on the back of the long church pew and Ollie in gratitude lifted his tail and squirted out a white stream from his rear end. He looked at the owl and said with a grin,

"Do a friend a favour and he fucks you," it was one of his favourite lines stolen from the tag line of one of Billy Connolly's jokes, and he thought very apt in view of the way people today treated each other. He put a kitchen wipe over the streak and left it to soak up the mess. Ollie shook himself, closed both eyes, and was to all intents and purposes asleep. "Little shit," the old man said under his breath, referring to the bird and not the streak.

Back in the comfort of his chair… one more sip of coffee and back to snooze time. The bookends ignored Ollie, the dogs ignored Ollie and Ollie was oblivious to all. The open fire spat out a small spark, the wall-eyed dog yawned and the old man closed his eyes for the third time and his dreams returned.

The dogs on the ledge were up and shaking off the water that had landed on them as they slept. It was time for their next move and as they left their last markings on the ledge the lead dogs started off, onwards and upwards towards the top of the ridge, where the bitch would decide which way to go.

They scrambled up the last part of the climb and without a second thought the bitch and her now stalwart companion were off at a steady, ground devouring lope that would take them far away to pastures greener and at least four valleys away. They would return to this well-known stomping ground but for now the imperative was to move. Her belly was once again full of newly starting life and she was heading for a more fertile environment to start her new family. The rest of the pack, loyal and trusting, followed.

She and her new found mate kept control. Her departure from the valley below would be welcomed by all - especially the old man, who had very little time for her or any other mixed blood pack. At least the true dingo was predictable; these packs of mixed domestic and wild dogs were a dangerous and fickle collection with no fear of man whatsoever.

It was another three days before the old man saddled up the stallion and started off to check on the whereabouts of the mares in the hills behind the Fairy Wood (which was now no longer there, as the fire had claimed it leaving nothing but charred ground.) It would regenerate in time, but would never be quite the same again. The rain was still steady and when he got to the river it was running quite quickly and all the debris left on its banks further upstream seemed to have been collected by the flow.

He didn't think there was any danger in crossing over; the water came up to just above the stallion's belly and he faced the lad upstream and walked him sideways across the current. That way he presented a chest and not a flank to the flow, reducing the chance of being swept off balance by the still fast running water. It also meant he would be able to see any bits of timber that might come out of nowhere, and have a chance of sidestepping them.

He had reached the far bank without mishap and stood for a moment to roll a cigarette and look up at the hillside just in case he might see the mares picking at any new shoots that might have sprung up with the rain. Not much up yet, he thought. Mark you, as soon as the rain stopped and the sun hit the now quite sodden ground, it wouldn't take long for the new growth to appear.

He lit up with the brim of his Akubra pulled down against the rain, shielding the lit paper between his lips. It was not enough protection and he spat the now wet strand of tobacco away into the rain, and they slowly set off across the river flats, his back to the charred remains of the old school house. He would see it in its entirety, or lack of, on his return, as he would be looking down on the remains all the way down from the top of the hill.

Time enough then for sadness and memories, right now, foremost on his mind were the mares, and the challenge of remaining upright as the ground was as slippery as ice. The stallion was as careful as he was observant and even though on occasions lost a hind foot, ending up in an exaggerated slip, was managing to keep a steady pace on the uphill climb. He had always marvelled at the way the stallion kept his balance.

He remembered one time when he was still riding competitive endurance races, setting off in the dark on a very wet and cold 3.00am start, going down a long and winding slope that was part of the Tenterfield Ride and feeling the stallion not lifting a foot, just skating down the track. ...And when in the light of day, doing the same track in reverse, marvelling at the length of the skid marks made by the sixty-odd open riders who had started off in the early morning. Many had not made it to the second leg of the ride as they had 'vetted out' after the first 40 km, either lame or metabolically stressed.

One had to be as fit as the horse you were mounted on as endurance riding was a gruelling sport. It was not just the monetary rewards that were an incentive, it was the fact that you saw parts of the countryside that others never had the chance of seeing, and had the incredible feeling of climbing high to the top of an otherwise inaccessible range, and coming out of the low cloud and mist to be engulfed in early morning sunshine. Looking back, the tree tops were poking out of the clouds below. You and your horse were now above, and the feeling of pure joy at the freedom of being so much higher than the fluffy white clouds that only moments ago were making you shiver.

Today, unfortunately, was a little different, as the clouds were dense and the rain was steady, and he was looking for lost friends with a slight feeling of foreboding. The horse, two dogs and the man kept climbing. The red dog was not as steady on her feet as the wall-eyed girl. Maybe he should have left her at home tied up in the comfort of her warm log kennel. With his head bowed against the rain, continually looking upward in the hope of catching sight of the mares, he continued his journey uphill, into the weather.

It was a long and arduous climb at the best of times and on this morning it seemed to be taking much longer than usual. He could just make out the big gums on the top ridge, all burnt and charred, their limbs no longer spreading out majestically; now more of a ghostly collection of dead and twisted timber that would eventually come crashing down and no longer grace the skyline that they had owned for so many years.

He was getting more and more worried as there were no swishing tails or sounds of galloping horses coming to see what he was up to. There were, unnervingly, the odd dead 'roo and other bits of unrecognisable carnage that the fire had left behind.

The dogs suddenly stopped, noses lifted upwards, testing the air. He stopped and waited for them to equate whatever the smell was and watched to see where they would head off to. He appreciated the breather, and so did the stallion, so they stood and waited while the dogs sifted out the scents that had got their attention. They were moving backwards and forwards now, not any great distance, just enough to get a line on the smells that their eager noses had picked up. Suddenly they turned away and started to pace off to the left, sideways across the hill. The old man gave the stallion his head and they followed the dogs, who brokc into a lopc and the horse picked up pace.

It was then that he saw them; he reined in and stood there quietly taking in the scene ahead. The dogs had reached their goal and were standing next to the mares. The old man's heart was coping with what his eyes were looking at and he slowly asked the horse to move on. The closer he got the more he could smell the odour that had originally got the dogs' attention.

The muscles in his thighs tightened and the stallion jumped forward. He spoke softly and the horse backed off; it had not been a command, it was a reaction to the picture that was unravelling in front of him. He did not want to get any closer, but he knew that he had no choice, the mares were all down and their bodies were bloated and disfigured. The closer he got the more his heart was praying that at the very least they had become overwhelmed by fumes and passed out before the flames had got to them. He could see the massive burn marks on their flanks and he felt the colour drain from his face.

...His dear, dear, old friend, the big and brave hearted mare that he had bred originally as a show jumper or even a three day eventer, but could never bring himself to sell on. They had bonded at an early age and had galloped their way over and sometimes through the biggest of obstacles. She did not know the meaning of propping up and stopping at a jump. If you asked her she would leap across the moon. His heart; oh God, he could feel his heart as it seemed to grow and nearly burst inside him; feelings not just for the mare but for the other two mares lying inert on the ground.

He had named the big mare Molly Maguire, after a film he had once seen about an Irish fighting family called the Maguire's, and she had all the same fighting qualities, bravery, stamina, a little foolhardiness, and to her friends she was as honest, kind and loving as a marshmallow melting in the mouth of a child. She was sixteen hands and one and a half inches to the top of her withers and probably in her hay day would have weighed in at 700 kilos at the very least. Yet she was gentle as a lamb, unless you were another horse competing for the attention that she firmly believed was for her alone, or a person that showed her no respect. To them, she was a spirit not to be underestimated. A powerhouse, who would have carried her knight into battle and if he had become unseated would have stood over him till the very end, such was her loyalty.

He could feel his heart pounding inside his chest; it felt as if it was going to break out and explode. The stallion felt it too and was unnerved by the passion in his friend and he wanted to move away. After all, this had been one of his mares; one of the mothers of his foals and it was all too complicated for him to take in. All he knew was that his friend was not happy and not at ease.

The journey back down the mountain was close to unbearable; not only did he carry the image of the dead mares within his heart, he was looking down on the non-existent Fairy Wood and a lone half-crumbled chimney across the swollen river that was all that was left of the old school house. The massive old camphor laurels that used to house the elaborate tree house had been nearly obliterated. He could remember the tree house packed with friends laughing at whatever it was that had caught their attention on the river flats below, be it a game of cricket or a stupid joke, it would never be heard again, it was all gone.

He was once more in his life experiencing a feeling of desolation and loneliness, a great and heavy loss. It was as if a large part of him was being left on the hillside and he would never fill the gap that was opening up in his heart. The stallion was dancing beneath him and he just sat there like a passenger on a fairground ride. The horse didn't go anywhere, he did not take off, he just danced on the spot as if desperately trying to put as much distance between him and what had upset his rider. His head was tucked up tight into his chest and his neck was curled up like a spring waiting to be unleashed at the slightest command, his feet slipping and sliding on the wet ground.

The old man's chin was ridged and his face was set, his eyes were jet black and cold - not out of anger - but with the strain of trying to control the emotion inside.

He got to the river, and stood there very still, very quiet, for what seemed like an eternity. He watched the water come and go leaving behind in the eddies the sharp eyed yabbies, which he would normally watch and marvel at. Today was different, he just watched the water and his tears joined the rain on his face and his heart broke.

When he eventually got home he towelled the horse dry in total silence, gave him a hard feed mixed with a little hot water and molasses, then he climbed wearily up to the veranda, opened the door and picked up the phone. Standing there, he cut a lonely figure, as the dogs had moved across to the hearth and were drying off in front of the fire, licking themselves.

He heard himself saying into the mouthpiece,

"Mate, when you reckon it's safe to take a 'dozer up onto the Fairy Hill can you turn off the track to the left, just before the big old rocks and dig a hole; you will know where, by the smell. It's the big old mare Molly and two others, they didn't make the fire. No, mate, 'fraid not. Well, we all know the saying, don't we, 'shit happens'. Thanks, appreciate that mate. I just don't want the dogs eating her out. When you finish up there come by and we can sink a rum or two; cool, I will see you when I see you. No, no, I'm fine and it's all part of life, eh, we come and we go. Thanks Buddy, catch you later."

And he went back inside putting the phone down and taking as deep a breath as he could, poured himself a stiff over-proof rum, no ice, just a warm burning sensation and he went back out onto the veranda to lean on the hand rail and let his heart go.

It was long past a dreary damp dawn before he realised that he had sat out all night. He had an old travelling rug over his knees and his long scarf wrapped round his neck. He hadn't even refilled his coffee from the night before. Whether he had dozed or not, he couldn't remember, all his thoughts were just a mish-mash in his head. The only realisation that stood out clearly was that if you cared for something or someone, eventually you would feel a hurt. Be it selfish, or be it a part of what was hidden deep inside of you, it would be painful in a way that cannot be described. And some sweet, loving person would tell you that you were being indulgent, or looking for attention; such was the way of some; usually those who thought that by adding to the pain you already felt they could score Brownie points. An animal will just nip or kick you, a human being will try to mess with your head and then put the blame on you, to hell with them all.

Then that sound of a grinding four-wheel drive coming along the bottom ridge started to register, and his thoughts started to change from melancholy to, 'Who the bloody hell is this?' It was Trevor, his CD player blaring out country music, with his rendition competing with the already overloud version of *Oh, Ruby, don't take your love to town.*

Ah, well, at the very least he would be forced into steak and eggs with mushrooms on the side, covered in butter.

"I came over the top ridge, mate, shit, she's as slippery as a politician's arse up there."

He swung his legs out of the Tojo and started to walk into the old forge with its lean to and hooks and chains and old-style blower that had kept many a hot furnace glowing over the years.

"I will grab the stallion - can you bring the youngster in and tie him up high and tight, let him get used to what's going on, then we can get stuck into a good eight ounce rib eye fillet, medium rare with mushrooms. Don't forget the mushrooms," and he was out of sight, still bloody singing, only to reappear with the old horse close on his heels and shaking his head, his mane flying all over the place and his front feet stepping high, angry that Trevor was ignoring his attempts at looking flashy on such a dull and grey old morning.

"Got the wind up his tail today, might just give him a minute to settle. Come on, grab the young colt and I'll tell you the news you will want to hear."

Trevor's idea of what you might or might not want to hear was whatever he had decided he would tell you anyway, such was his nature, and most times he was right. Even when he wasn't, it was informative and interesting; they had known each other too long to worry about whether or not things should be said or not said, they just came out with it, and that was that.

"The dog pack has gone; their sign is all across the top ridge. There are dingoes up there to full blood, or as close to it, and some domestic dumped dogs as well. I reckon they will all join up and that old bitch will have herself quite a pack by the time she reaches her destination, which if I'm not mistaken will be on the far side of Murrey's Run. And there is more game and stray cattle out there than they could ask for in a month of Sundays, they won't need for anything and with a bit of luck they will stay there for a long, long, time. That is if the piggers and their tough tooth and nail dogs don't flush them out.

"I don't see Molly Maguire down here - shame that - I could of trimmed her up before this wet got into those big plates of meat you call feet."

"No, not here;" a lost look appeared on the old man's face, "She was up on top of the Fairy Wood hill."

"Shit, there won't be much feed up there after the fire, old mate - you'll have to bring her back down to the river flats till the shoots come through."

"Not part of the game plan, I'm afraid, Trevor, she didn't make the fire."

"Oh, bugger old mate, I am so sorry, well, I am just hoping that the smoke and the fumes knocked her out before the flames got to her."

"I found her yesterday with two other mares; not pretty, not pretty at all. I've asked Johnny to take his dozer up there and dig a hole, he reckons it will climb anything, so that should be done by the weekend."

"Well, I gotta tell you, I thought you looked a bit rough; that explains it, big loss old mate, Hey, do you remember when I had her hind foot nearly up to her chest trying to get that bloody old twisted shoe off her? And she just pulled me back underneath her as if to say, 'So, think you are strong, eh? This is strong you silly old bastard' - and then the old prick pissed on me."

The old man started to grin,

"She was only about five then, she was a big mare alright, and, old mate, I'll never forget the day she booted you. What was she - four months old - caught you on the inside of your thigh just below the family jewels; remember, you came in and we had steak and you forgot the mushrooms and after breakfast about an hour later, I reckon, you got up from the table, never said a word, and off you went into the paddock, got hold of the small tie rope on her halter, lined her up and booted her fair and square in the guts. Do you remember what you said to her?"

"Nope, can't say I do."

"Well let me tell you, the exact words were, and I quote, 'Don't ever think you will get too big for me to kick you back.' And you came into the house rubbing your hands together and said 'that will teach her.' I don't think I've ever laughed so much, she wouldn't have even felt it, you silly old fool."

"Hey, hey, settle down now. It wasn't the kick, mate, it was her pride I was aiming for, just letting her know she wasn't the Queen Bee that she thought she was."

"Have it your own way, mate, I lived off that story for weeks."

And Trevor winked and laughed out loud,

"Right mate, let's get this old boy done and then we can spend a bit of time on the colt, before we get stuck into breakfast."

Trevor had tied the colt's front leg up tight to his belly and onto a strap tied to his wither. It would become not only stiff, but also a little numb and keep his mind on balancing, rather than fighting the farrier, as he trimmed and rasped with precision and an expert eye, rounding off the front of the hoof and correcting the slight imperfection of the straightness of the leg; nothing much now, but if left it could just make the difference between slight lameness or not, in the future. Could this be called corrective shoeing? Who knows, there were so many different names for common sense these days, just to make a person look as if they knew what they were doing. Best to say nothing and be known as someone who never seemed to have any problems with the horses that they managed, so much better than crowing over one's own work; that usually led to people trying to knock the work or bring you down.

That was a favourite of people who never really did much except to think that by knocking someone else they made themselves look good. So much better to start one's day off with a bright thought than, 'who shall we criticise and tear apart this morning?' The old man had listened to far too much of that over the years, and all that it did was make the person handing out the crap more miserable than they were in the first place. He laughed lightly, and Trevor looked at him and shook his head as if to say 'silly old prick what on earth are you dreaming of now?'

Both the horses were done and back in their respective stables, and the two men were climbing the steps to the veranda. Trevor unbuckled his thick leather chaps that he had favoured for years now instead of the standard farriers apron, and headed for the sink to scrub up. The old man put the cast iron frying pan on the combustion stove, the firebox of which was filled with well-seasoned hard wood so that when he put the steak in, it would sizzle and seal the outside of the meat keeping all the wonderful juices held inside only to run out across the plate at the first cut. You can't beat a properly cooked piece of fillet, especially when joined with two eggs that were deep in colour and texture; free range and horse feed fed. Add to this heavily buttered toast, fresh mushrooms and raw tomatoes, a never-ending pot of freshly ground coffee and good company and you had the makings of a perfect morning. There was no tomato sauce or Lee and Perrins, just black peppercorns in a grinder and melting in the mouth meat. Oh, the joys of simple living, plates cleaned with a piece of home baked bread collecting any left-over juices and then more than squeaky clean, placed in the sink. So now it was time for more coffee and good conversation.

"Shame about the big mare,"

"Well, Trevor, it was a sad day yesterday, tomorrow will be better, and then it will become a dull memory. We know it won't really, but that is the only way one can look at it and stay sane.

"It sort of makes that young colt a very special project; I think he is quite a bright sort of bloke - just young and a bit full of himself, so, what's your opinion, Trevor, on his attitude to becoming a horse proper, or do you think he will become just another dizzy Arabian Cross?"

"He is by the old stallion isn't he, and out of that big mare. Mate, I reckon if he doesn't blow up he will make whatever you want him to be; he has all the potential you could want, all we need to know now is does he have a brain? A lot of the ones I used to show all those years ago were as flashy as all hell but not a brain between them; all prance and prick. If there was a matchstick on the road they would fall over it, bloody hopeless, hey, fill that up will you mate, then I better make a move, got to make the money to pay the tax man, heh,heh,heh."

"You might make it, Trev, but I don't think the tax man ever sees much of it."

"Come on now, what was it Kerry Packer once said, 'if you make it and then give it away to the taxation department then you are a bigger fool than your accountant, and him you can fire.'

"Mate, you only pay out what the minimum is that you have to, a philanthropic patriarch I am not, three boys, a wife and a farm, I support my own, not a road that's still dirt and drains that don't work, or a hospital that closes beds down at the drop of a political hat. A bit like the statement, 'there are less people on the dole this first quarter,' of course there are - the politicians moved them over to sickness and job start, they must think we're all bloody stupid, maybe we should all go to lunch at parliament house, or better still, go surfing and drinking on their tax. It's all bullshit, old man, and you know it just as well as I do. Once you are no more use to the powers that be, you are just a number. It's the politicians' perks, mate - and don't they abuse them - being a bencher back or front is a great job as long as you go with the flow and only answer a direct question if it is phrased the way the manual says it has to be, anyway, you should know, eh, we are still getting the same price for our cattle as we were twenty years ago, only the yard fees have gone up, the price of feed has doubled and we don't get cheap fuel anymore.

"But old mate, I don't see the menu at Parliament House being cut back - they still eat far better than most and get paid for doing so. So I will keep on doing what I do and keeping what I keep. The government will get it off me in the end, with some 'how dare you die now?' tax, you just wait and see.

"Well, the time has come, got to make a move, can't have too much fun knocking the powers that be, or they'll hit us with a laughter tax. See you in a month, unless you need me or I feel like a good breakfast. Take it easy, and I'm really sorry about Molly; some good old memories, mate, that's what we live on at our age."

The Tojo left the yard with the gears crunching and the vocals: always the same when he left, "Oh, Lord, it's hard to be humble, when you're perfect in every way."

One thing about Trevor, what you saw was what you got, and if you missed the rogue in him then you got caught as well. They were good mates, but the game was the game, and they played it well.

The old man had a really close mate in surfers' paradise who over the years had met Trevor and he always said,

"Mate, that Trevor would have been one hell of a larrikin when he was younger, 'cause he's one hell of a bullshitter now. He's a very clever old boy that one is, and you are very lucky to have him as a mate… I would hate to have him as anything else."

And George, being an old Melbourne boy from a Greek family, was a pretty smart streetwise sort of a bloke. He and the old man had been mates forever - it would be 40 years now. George loved the bush to visit, but not to live in.

"Too bloody rural for me," was what he used to say, "Gotta be able to eat sushi or Italian or go game fishing and all within 15 minutes of each other. So visiting is great, and going home is even better."

His kids didn't agree, but after maybe a week of being woken at 4.00 am by an over happy rooster they would be asking to go back to surfers and seagulls that didn't crow. He laughed out loud and looked around to see if anyone was looking, then laughed again as he remembered that whenever he had come off a horse in the bush in the middle of nowhere, without a soul for miles and miles, the very first thing he always did was look around to see if anyone had seen him fall. We all feel stupid at the craziest of times, and this was no exception.

It was nearly midday before he put the colt into the round yard. It would be an easy lesson today, not just because of the weather, he wanted the new shoes the colt was wearing to bed in as gently as possible and let him get used to that little extra weight on his foot.

Also he was preoccupied with sadness and a feeling of great loss. He and Molly Maguire would never again share a soft muzzle or a walk in the early morning, her pushing him along with that big block head, or just leaning her bony chin on his shoulder; hearing her whinny a greeting when she saw him walking towards her or the thundering of her big feet as she galloped at him - only to prop up just before what looked like a total disaster was about to happen - and skid to a halt blowing out through pursed lips, making a sound he would never forget. And those soft lips taking his fingers and looking for the treat that she knew he would have hidden somewhere in a pocket or in his hand…

Enough of this, he thought to himself, the past is the past and tomorrow would hold new, and, oh hell, who was he kidding, all the tomorrows he had been through all ended up the same; whatever he loved he outlived, and the pain was getting more and more hard to bear and the memories were getting less and less. As he got older, life became more occupied with what had gone before; what was left was his chair, and the time to think, not always the best remedy for an aching heart, but a lot better than a bottle of whisky and a head full of remorse.

He unclipped the lunge rope and led the colt out to one of the day yards, to hell with going round in circles, he needed to walk out into the fields and just sit for a while; feel the earth beneath him and the breeze on his cheek, chew a piece of grass and look into the distance and get lost in the blur and the shimmer of old tired eyes that had probably seen more than was good for the brain over the years.

After a shorter lesson than was originally planned he put the young colt away and gave him a feed and a bit of a rub on the flank. He might even lie down on Mother Earth and close his eyes for a while and let her fill him with her power and a little peace. This day for him was done and he would walk back to the house when the chill of the evening forced him to move. He must have dozed off, because it was a dog's soft tongue that woke him and the early mist had started to float across the flats. He raised himself on one elbow and winced just a little as the pain in the small of his back bought him back to reality.

"Bugger," he said and rose slowly onto one knee, looking back at the farm house and realising that he had to do the final feed and lock up the chickens, the firewood, did he have enough inside? God, surely he could remember such a basic little thing as is there enough cut wood next to the Aga and the fireplace?

Ah,well, he would soon find out.

Come on girls, he said under his breath and the three of them walked slowly back to the yard. He placed a light rug on the colt, fresh water, a biscuit of Lucerne hay and a small, yet non-heating hard feed. He did the same for the stallion only he put him in his day yard; it was a pleasant night and the rain had gone, and there was a full moon. He put a fractionally heavier rug on the stallion and let him out to enjoy the night and a little full moon madness.

Locking up the chooks he saw that there were a few young cockerels that could easily lose their heads tomorrow and end up in the freezer before they became a nuisance and started bracing up to his old rooster. He chuckled, old, he was only two and in his prime; next year he would probably be in the stew pot for his sins, and a new boy would be on the block giving his chickens the run around. He was toying with the idea of either a very game bantam rooster or one of those gangly game birds that added leg and breast to the average chook.

Enough, he thought, time to get inside and give the fire a bit of a poke and start his evening off with a few sparks and a bit of a crackle. I might even watch the news, just to keep in the know, so to speak. He climbed the stairs and light briefly flooded out onto the veranda as he opened the door to his inner sanctum.

He shouldn't have fallen asleep flat out on the dirt like that. It was still damp from the rain and he had lain there for a good four hours, just enough time to put a chill in his bones. A large whisky, some honey, a splash of lemon juice and a drop of hot water, well, it was a good excuse for a toddy wasn't it? This done and his black coffee sitting next to him on the round table, he hit the remote and the TV screen changed from blank to vaguely informative.

There was a time when he would have the TV on all the time just so there was motion happening in the room, a cast off from all those days and nights spent in hotels around the world when he was working. He was thinking back to those days when a picture of an old mate came on the screen with the words 'died at the age of 73 at his home early this morning after losing his battle with cancer and a recent stroke'. Coming from the TV like that was so impersonal and his attention was completely taken up with yet another mate's demise.

The phone started ringing almost immediately and as he managed to get a quick yes out of his mouth, the voice on the other end was saying,

"Have you seen the news, there's another one gone, not many of us left now, are there?"

"Did I need reminding of that," the old man said into the mouthpiece. "Don't you think that I am all too well aware that Old Nick is just waiting to have the last laugh?"

"Oh. Sorry old mate," said the very British voice on the other end. "I just wanted to touch base and have a word."

"No, no, my stuff up," he said, "I shouldn't have been so abrupt, it's just that I lost one of my mares this week; a bit of a special girl she was - and then turning on the television I was a bit taken off guard, sorry, old mate, take no notice of me, just a bit edgy, that's all. You should drive down and stay for a couple of days, let me take some dosh off you at backgammon, and we could talk about the living and what pricks they all are."

They both laughed and agreed that he should cruise down in a week or so. So many Brits living in Australia now, every actor and muso either hit L.A. or they recluse themselves in Aus. Some bought farms and commuted to work when the job demanded it, or they lived in Sydney, Melbourne or the Queensland coastline. The phone went dead and the old man left it off the cradle; he knew if he didn't it would keep ringing late into the night. A death always meant people would ring, he figured it was to prove to the caller that they were still alive, due mainly to the fact that their call had been answered.

He remembered when Shirley from the Skyhooks had flown his plane upside down into the ground, there had been a heap of them when the call came through; old mates sitting in the Green Room at Channel Nine in Melbourne, waiting to fill their guest spots on a TV games show. Funny how many people feared death, yet to him it was just a part of life and was going to catch us all one day, some of us sooner than others.

The television had moved unceremoniously onto the weather so he left it alone to see what the report had in store for the next week. Refilling his coffee he thought, 'long range weather report they call it, they don't even know how deep the ocean is in some places, how on earth did they expect us to believe that they knew what Mother nature had in store for us in four days' time. It was about 11.30 when he turned off the TV. There had been situation comedies back to back and then a Carry On film and they all had old mates of his in them so he had watched and smiled to himself remembering days from a bygone era.

The two dogs were standing by the door and obviously wanted to go out into the night. He opened the door, and followed them out. The dogs went down the steps, the wall-eyed dog at quite a speed, the red dog still a bit wobbly, but seeming in command of most of her body. It was just her hind quarter that seemed to trip up a bit but that would pass. The moon was big and bright and lit up the whole yard, the stallion was in his day yard, nibbling the last little bits of Lucerne, completely relaxed and seemingly at peace with the world. The moon had that blueish ring around it, not a tinge to it, more a containing circle that suggested rain.

He was feeling a bit brighter, watching old mates on the television and going back in time had just lifted him a little. Squint had come back to the veranda and was sitting by the door waiting for him to open it; he whistled for the red dog and looked out at the yard below. There was no sign of movement. She had probably gone round to the barn to catch up on the mouse and rat movement.

He opened and closed the door as quickly as possible, knowing she would scratch on it when she was ready to come in. The chair beckoned, and he slumped into it, the bookends were out mousing or even looking for a rabbit - they tended to go a bit crazy on the full moon. Life was so easy if you didn't complicate it; his eyes started to close and moonlight flooded into the room and joined the fire in an eerie sort of glow.

NINETEEN
A Parting

It would have been around 6am when he jolted upright. He arched his back and felt a twinge, coffee will sort it out. It was then that he realised that the red dog still wasn't inside. Bugger, I must have slept through her scratching's, never mind, she could curl up in a corner of the veranda and be quite snug, all good, no problems there.

He opened the door, coffee in hand and Squint scampered down the steps for her morning ablutions. He rested on the hand rail and looked at the morning, the red dog wasn't on the veranda; she had probably gone back to the barn in disgust at his lack of interest. Even warmer, there, he thought, all that lovely straw to languish in.

Back inside for another cup of coffee and maybe toast, yes, why not, with thick orange peel marmalade , then he would open up the colt's top door, bring the stallion in from his yard and take off the rugs and give both horses a good grooming and a mandatory chat. Yes, the day was going to be OK, a bit of positive thinking and some round yard work and then lunch.

He sauntered down to the colt's stable with a bit of a spring in his step, opened up the top door and threw in a small biscuit of hay; the Lucerne treat was yesterday and this morning the shredded hay was just to get his gut juices working, then grooming, then the round yard, a quick strap down and a hard feed.

Anybody who thought this horse business was easy needed their head examined, then again, it was well worth the effort when you looked at the end result. He turned his attention to the stallion's day yard and walked across to see what was what; a good phrase that covered a myriad of meanings.

"Well, I'll be," he said as he saw the red dog lying in the middle of the yard with the stallion standing next to her, "An early morning chat between mates."

It was then that he felt the hairs on the back of his neck start to rise; all was not well, something was amiss, she had not got up, nor had she wagged her tail as was her normal activity when he approached. And the stallion had not whinnied or even given a small nicker of greeting.

He increased his speed and climbed between the third and fourth rail, then stood very still, in fact he could not move even if he had wanted to. He was fixed in the space that he stood in, the red dog had not moved and her position was all wrong, and there was a strange, dull discoloured area at the top end of her head. No, oh, please, no, the old man knew what blood looked like only too well, he had seen enough of it from a very early age. He tried to move forward, but his legs would not respond; he lent forward, and to stop himself falling, self-preservation took over and his left leg moved forwards, followed by his right, and then he was there. He looked down at the inert body and he felt numb; his legs were like lead and they buckled and he went to his knees. The stallion never moved, he also just stood there, they must have looked like three tragic statues, horse, man and a red dog who was obviously dead. His hand was shaking as he placed it on the dog's neck. She was stiff; in the final stages of rigour mortis. The top of her scalp was not joined to anything, it was its own piece of matter. It had been clean shaven from her head and the blood had seeped out and was now a dried, congealed stain on the ground.

He was very nearly sick, somehow he managed to rise and very slowly went to the feed shed, picked up a hessian bag and on returning to the scene, gently covered the dog up with the sack; got hold of the stallion's head collar and walked him back to his stable, threw in a biscuit of hay and lent against the stable door.

"What now, what bloody now?" He went back to the feed shed and picked up a shovel and a crow bar and a mattock, put them in a wheelbarrow and headed back to the day yard.

He looked at the small lean to shelter attached to the yard just in case of rain and rested the three items against the slab wall. Then he went back to the feed shed again and picked up the pick with the double blade - a sharp end and a large splayed blade on the other end. Putting it over his shoulder he carried it back to the yard and as he lent it up against the railings he felt his legs buckle slightly.

The lean-to was about fourteen feet deep and he hit the ground dead centre with the crow bar and the first piece of dirt flaked off. He then looked at it lengthwise and made an indentation at either end with the spade, then joined up the two ends with a line along the dirt.

Next he took up the pick and slowly started to hit the ground with the pointed end to break up the surface. He then shovelled the loose dirt out of the hole and placed it in a pile just to the left of his digging. He took off his scarf and his sweater, rolled up his sleeves and started to dig in a very matter of fact manner, breaking the dirt and shovelling it out, as though he was on a factory assembly line.

It was a good two hours before he had finished and the grave was about three feet deep at least and two feet wide and probably four feet long. He was being as methodical as he could under the circumstances; his breathing was not as regular as he would have liked it to be and he found himself gasping at times. The sun was beating down; not like a full-on summer's day, but enough to make him sweat, and he knew that he must drink water now or feel the consequences later. He had gone to the tap half a dozen times and put his mouth over the spout as he had already forgotten where he had put his coffee cup.

It was of no importance, his whole being was focussed on the resting place for his friend and his mind was not concerned with lost cups or the pain in his back and legs. All his attention was placed on not letting his mind wander from the task at hand, finish digging and then cope with the next exercise on the agenda.

One thing at a time, it was the only way that he would be able to complete this dig. Think of nothing else than what he was doing at that particular moment; easy, if it wasn't important, it wasn't worth thinking about. So there was no choice, one foot after the other, as the saying goes.

He had taken a bucket of water over to the hessian sack and poured it on top. He didn't want the heat of the sun to start a smell; he had also taken out the knife from its sheath on his belt and put his hand under the sack and cut into the belly of the dog to release the gases that had started to build up as he didn't want her to swell, either. It was all done methodically and with precision; whatever was happening in his head or his heart must not get in the way of what had to be done.

How he would cope later was an unknown factor at the moment. Going back once again into the yard was more than painful, and so it was with a heavy heart that he walked up to the house, climbed the steps and found the blanket that only a week ago the red dog had lain upon in the chair as the tick's poison was carried through her body.

With the blanket in his hand he walked slowly back to the lifeless body of a friend that once placed in the grave he had dug, he would only ever see again in his dreams. He knelt down and cradled the stiff and hapless form, his legs buckling slightly from the pain that was now much worse since the dig. He got to the rails and stood very still, as if not wanting to relinquish the body for one second. He could not squeeze through the rails without putting her down on the ground and then he pulled the hessian under the bottom rail until she was through. Then he bent down and once more cradled the body tightly to his chest and walked the dozen or so paces to the grave.

Taking the hessian and placing it on the bottom of the freshly dug hole, he then put her blanket, single folded on top of the sack. Ever so gently he laid the red dog to rest, covering her up with the other half of the worn old blanket that recalled so many memories. And very slowly he stood up and started to shovel back the earth. There was no ceremony or words said as the dirt fell on the blanket, he just shovelled and shovelled and shovelled till the grave was filled and then he went and filled the wheelbarrow with rocks which he placed very carefully on top of the slight mound that was all there was to see of what had once been a red dog with a lolling tongue and pricked up ears.

He would in a few days' time find a white rose that he would plant on the top of the mound, but for now, just finishing the job at hand was enough of an ordeal for any man, let alone him. He put the shovels and the mattock, the pick and the crowbar back into the barrow and pushed it back to the feed room. Going next to the tack room he picked up a hard and a soft brush and headed for the stallion's stable.

He must start grooming, maybe the young colt first. Yes, that was what he would do; he placed the stallion's brushes on the mounting block next to the old horses stable and went back to the tack room to get the young horse's brushes and slowly went into his stable and after clipping the colt to the hook on the wall brushed him down in complete silence. When he had finished he got his feed and refreshed his water, leaving the top of his stable door open and clipped back.

He then went into the stallion's stable, clipped him to a lower hook than he had for the colt, and pulling the hoof pick out of his pocket, picked up his front feet and started to clean them out. It was when he picked up his off-side hind foot that he saw the darkish stain on the top of the hoof and he now knew which foot it was that had clipped the top of the red dog's skull and laid it bare. He dipped a rag into the water container and cleaned the stain off the hoof.

Then he started to brush the horse down, there was no malice in him as he brushed along the horse's neck. There would have been a perfectly reasonable explanation as to why the kick had been delivered. And it was as he always said, history was unchangeable. What was done was done and life would go on, only not for the red dog, she was gone and under the ground and that was that.

He lent on the stallion's back and felt weak and for the first time, old and very tired. The stallion fluttered his nostrils and turned his head into the man's side, pushing him very gently, as if to say, 'I'm so very, very sorry.' The old man stroked his neck and unclipped him from the hook, refilled his water container and went out to get his feed. Then, as with the colt he clipped back the top door and slowly made his way back to the homestead. His feet had lost their bounce and it seemed as if it was a great effort to put one foot in front of the other. The wall-eyed dog was close on his heel; so close in fact that his chin got knocked by the back of the old man's boot, and the dog slowed down his pace just a fraction.

The young colt started to speak but the stallion cut him off abruptly,

"Don't ask, just listen," he said. "I was dozing and as you know we the horse never sleep completely. I was thinking of the big mare, your dam, your mother, and one of my mares. She was taken by the smell that filled our noses when the flames were here. It choked her and she will never leave the hillside. You will never see her again and I was not there to lead her to safety.

"And now, as I remember it, it was while I was thinking of her that a shadow crossed behind me as I nodded in my yard. It passed between me and the light from the sky. Purely from instinct I kicked out with my back leg and when I turned round it was the red dog and not a foe. The red dog is no more and my friend the old man is sad and so am I. So I am going to stand with my head in a corner and I am not going to speak again. Until I do you will not speak to me and we will be silent and I will lower my head for I am tired. There will be vibration and sound coming through the roof timber; it will be the old man, he will need to listen and so will we."

He turned and put his head into the corner and the colt dared not make a sound as sadness enveloped them both.

The old man reached the steps and started to climb; his legs were heavy and he ached from top to bottom. When he reached the veranda he turned and looked back at the yard, grasping the hand rail and leaning as he never had before. The muscles in his arms pained him greatly from digging and the rest of him was a mess.

He went inside and made his way to the first aid box that his doctor always made sure was filled with what he might need if he cramped up or hurt himself. Here was a packet of diazepam used to release a tired and strained muscle. It would be his back or the top of his legs, he very seldom took them as he did not like the feeling of not knowing how much it hurt. If he could feel the pain then he would not do any more damage. He took three 5ml tablets then one more just to clinch the outcome which hopefully would be a release, of what, he wasn't sure.

Then he picked up the liquid morphine. This was there not to kill the pain; it just moved it to one side and gave it a different perspective. He had never really bothered with measures and he also stayed away from the mixture, but today was different and he shook the bottle and took what can only be described as a swig.

He filled his coffee cup and went back out onto the veranda, held onto the railing once again and wept with no sound at all. He just wept; he felt like a rag doll, his body was screaming out and his head was even worse and the tears poured out of his eyes and down his face like rivers. There was no respite; only emotional turmoil; he could not turn left or right, forwards or backwards - there was nowhere left to go. His whole being was taken over by an overwhelming feeling of despair. He had lost himself to himself and there was nothing left to lean on. He was deeper than he had ever been before… lost in a place that had no boundaries; there was nothing to keep him in.

He felt himself going backwards and then sitting, and he wept, his body shaking uncontrollably. The wall-eyed dog moved inside - she was scared by what she felt coming from the old man; his power had dissolved, his shields were down and she had no red dog to push up against. The bookends were uneasy and growled and spat at each other and the old man wept and the two horses below stood with their heads buried in the corners of their stables.

Somehow through all this the old man knew he must get inside, how he would get there, he didn't know as his legs were no longer a part of him. He went forwards onto his knees and crawled into the house. His body pushed the door shut. He had to get control, of what he didn't know, he just knew his weakness would kill him. Never ever show weakness.

He went to the fireplace and filled it with logs then he dragged the fireguard in front of the fire and placed the two big cast iron stew pots in front of the guard so that even if a log dislodged it would not knock it over. And he wept; he managed to get to his feet, everything was such an effort.

He knew he had maybe half an hour before the diazepam would kick in and he must be safe before that happened. He put CDs in the stacker without even looking at the titles. It did not matter, everything he had was part of him, part of life from before until now. He was alone, he had been alone before, he had been alone in a crowd. Yet this was different. The music started and he realised that he wasn't weeping for himself, he was weeping for Molly and the red dog and his friends that were no more. The red dog would never lie in front of the open fire with him rubbing liniment into her rheumatism, or tweaking her ear. She, like Molly, had gone without him being with her, she had gone, all alone.

He slumped into his chair and wept, and the pain in his chest came in a wave. He was exhausted, so tired, so much pain and he felt the diazepam releasing the muscles in his back and the morphine was putting the pain in another place and yet he hurt deep down inside. He could hear a voice calling him but he didn't recognise it.

"Get a grip you old fool," he heard himself say. "Who will feed the horses if you don't, who will let the bookends out, who will put the white rose on the red dog's grave, who will…" and he passed out from the stabbing pain that seemed to take his body and hurl it at the wall. It was as though his whole being had fragmented.

Even though he had lost consciousness the music was there inside him and all his past and present was fighting with the future. And somewhere in there was his essence, his very being fighting to stay, fighting to be. Now it was up to what was inside him as to whether he survived or not, how much strength did he have left? He was cradled by his chair and now only time would tell.

Squint had, on that fateful night, gone down the veranda steps at a rate of knots. The red dog had been slower; the tick's poison had left, but there were consequences: the hind quarters seemed to overtake her front end - she had a recurring wobble.

She reached level ground and headed for the barn, passing the stallions yard; she would pay him a visit on her way back. Right now she was intent on whatever mysteries the old barn might hold. She entered the barn slowly and stealthily; there was always the chance of surprising a venturing rat. She stopped and drank in every little waft that came to her sensitive nose; nothing much here, she thought, then lifted her nose and drank in the night. What she could smell was another of those incredibly stupid chickens who had laid her eggs between two bales of hay at the back of the barn. The hen had left the security of the hen house to take her chances with hungry rats or even a game young fox.

The red dog moved away, and headed for the old Massey Ferguson, a relic of tractors from the past. The old man used it to turn the wheel of the chaffing machine that once a month he set in motion to make up his mixture of Lucerne, barley and paddock hay, his favourite mix to add to the horses' hard feeds. What fell on the barn floor gave the chooks good scratching material and the odd mouse could always find some seeds of interest - usually before a patient bookend pounced.

The red dog skirted the tractor, but her rear end wobbled and back legs crossed in an ungainly manner and she bounced into the tractor wheel - which ended any surprise she had intended for an unsuspecting rodent. She growled, more at herself than anything else; as with all animals, they hate imperfections that hamper their natural instincts.

As she had blown her cover, she went back out to the yard; the moon was behind her as she slipped under the bottom rail of the stallion's day yard and she headed towards his sleeping form, the clips on his rug shining in the light of the moon. She was within four feet of her friend when her back end gave way and she growled with the pain that her swerve had caused her spine. And that was the last thing she ever knew, as the stallion's newly shod hoof came striking out of nowhere. When the stallion turned round to inspect what he thought was an attacker, he was puzzled by the form on the ground; it didn't occur to him that he was the cause of the red dog's demise–that fact was yet to come. Now he stood over her as if guarding the body of his friend.

TWENTY
A Rousing

In his stable, the stallion woke with a start, turned around from his dark corner and faced the early morning's chill. The top door to his stable was still on a latch and wide open. This was not the only unusual greeting to his day, the music from the homestead was not a morning sound, it was more of a late afternoon sound and not in keeping with the norm. He felt uneasy and he could not explain the feeling.

"Colt," he said loudly, "Colt," there was a stirring in the next door stable. "Do not question me, do not say one word, just do as I tell you."

This was a statement and not a request.

"I want you to kick your bottom stable door just where the piece of wood goes across it low down to the floor.

"Do it with your front feet and change them over; also rattle the feed bin on your door with your nose. You manage to make enough din when you are eating so that should not be a problem for you, and don't stop until I tell you to or until I stop. Got that?"

"Yes sire," came the reply.

"Well at least he got that bit right, so, start now!" And the two horses young and old kicked their stable doors and rattled their feed bins.

As for the old man, his body was in a totally relaxed state due to the medication, the day had turned to night and back to day again. The fire had become glowing embers by the time he came to. He felt sluggish and a little disorientated yet he knew exactly where he was, but wasn't sure why. Slowly his brain started to focus and he remembered the pain and the fact it had been bad enough to take strong pain killers - something that he usually resisted.

He sighed and realised that the wall-eyed dog was waiting at the door which meant he must have been out of it for quite a while. He eased himself out of the chair and let the dog out, she wagged her tail and leapt down the veranda steps and off into her favourite spots marking her territory with urgency.

The old man went to the fire and raked the still faintly lit embers so that small sparks flew upward towards the chimney stack and he placed some small timber strategically across the glowing embers at just the right angle to catch light without smothering the flame. The wood began to crackle away as the outer bark caught alight and became a small source of heat again. Coffee, he thought and then realised that the Aga was out and had to be relit. Well, a billy on the open fire would do for his first cup until the slow combustion came back to life again.

The sound of the door kicking was not the first alarm - it was the feed bins clanging away that penetrated his thoughts, and a vision of a young colt, having reared up for some reason and had somehow got his leg in the metal bin and was tearing away at his tendon in sheer panic.

He rose from the chair, placed his coffee on the side and opening the door called out,

"OK, OK, OK, cut it out, I'm coming," and taking his 'Dry as a bone' from behind the door started down the steps in the half light of morning, the fog in his head slowly clearing as the cold air tightened the skin on his scalp and made his ears ache. His stride lengthened as the urgency of the situation became clearer. His only thought was for the young colt in panic and ripping away at his front legs to free them from the bin, he had seen it happen before and it was not a pretty sight.

The noise had stopped. He arrived at the stable door and the young colt was obviously agitated and circling round and round in his fourteen by fourteen stable. At first glance there seemed to be no damage.

Surely not the old stallion, he has too much sense? He moved across to the stallion's door and there he saw a horse blanket still on, and salty sweat lines all down his neck. The cold of the morning suddenly hit him with a lung-grabbing tightness; he entered the stable quickly and closed the bottom door behind him. The old horse nickered and blew out through his nostrils.

"I'll be damned," the old man said to himself as he looked down at the cross beam on the door and saw the newly splintered pieces of timber freshly made and hanging off the plank of wood. The feed bin was now only hanging onto the top of the door with one L-shaped handle.

So, why the racket, he wondered. It hadn't occurred to him that somehow the horses knew that he should be woken. He went to the tack room and came back with two brushes and a bucket of lukewarm water, a sponge and a towel, and taking off the stallion's rug started to groom his old mate. He went slowly and methodically over the horse's body, every now and then leaning on him to get his breath and let his aching muscles relax a bit.

His logic was that the continual sweeping of his arms from side to side, holding the brush in one hand and the sponge in the other, was good for him as it stretched out his chest, increasing the oxygen flow. He spent a long time on the old horse and had contemplated going back to the house for a coffee before starting on the colt, but realised that if he did, he might nod off in any one of his chairs, as a feeling of weariness had suddenly come over him. So he went straight on to cleaning up the young colt, more lukewarm water, the colt's own brushes (he never used one horse's cleaning stuff on another just in case of cross infection of any skin condition).

Off came the young bloke's rug, and as a late thought he clipped his head stall up to one of the higher hooks on the stable wall. The one day, if he forgot, would be the day he got kicked. There was an old saying that you often got hurt by someone else's horse in someone else's yard, doing them a favour. Very true, but then again, why tempt fate, it could just as easily happen at home. So he always tied his horses up while handling them in the stable or the yard, a habit learned by experience, and of course, being kicked.

The younger horse was much more agitated than the stallion; mainly because he had no understanding of what the older horse had meant by making all this noise with the stable door and the feed bins. It had not occurred to him that the noise was to wake the old man and get him out of the house and down to where the old horse believed he should be.

This had no relevance at all in the younger horse's reasoning; he was just learning the rules of what he was supposed to do within his own boundaries, which were determined by his peers. He appeared to be governed by not another horse, but by a man, a man who somehow had control not just of his future but his very existence. He also had complete and utter sanction of the stallion, who also, by his own means, seemed to have some control over the man.

Too many confusing circles for this young colt to get his head around, so agitation, confusion, and then the realisation of how good that brush felt as it gently but firmly caressed his back, only then to tickle, not so much annoyingly, but with a discomfort that was actually quite pleasant as it ran along his girth line and then deeper and with determination along his belly. It made him pick up a hind leg and just let it hang and quiver in mid-air, and then once again, he twisted his mouth and nostrils completely out of shape for no apparent reason at all except that he did. Just like his mother had always said to him. It does because it can and because it can, it does. He did not really understand it then and he didn't understand it now, he just did it. More confusion, only he had to admit it was bloody good and he loved it to a point where he felt as if he craved it…and then all of a sudden it had stopped.

Stopped, finished, gone, the old man was nowhere to be seen; and the door to his stable was closed and he was no longer tied to the wall. The stallion, the only source of information, was snoring loudly as only a horse can. The colt was livid, but he dared not wake the old horse; nothing left to do except wait till he was summoned.

The old man stood away from the stables yet not too close to the day yards, and he surveyed the rails and the mound of earth in the middle of the slabs on the side of the lean to stable. Dampened by the night's dew it looked slightly bigger than it had the night before. He wanted so desperately to see the red dog walk away into the now sunlit yard. He would find exactly the right rose that would climb up and along the slabs and eventually cover the side of the lean to - and all from the goodness of the red dog's spirit that lay beneath the ground.

He spun on his heel and went back to the veranda, coffee, and maybe, much as he hated to admit it, give the doctor a ring just to have him come out and look him over. He felt as though he had been run over by a Mack truck, then again, if that was all that was wrong with him, well, he could cope with that. He sat on the veranda for a long spell and the wall-eyed dog lay at his feet seemingly no more troubled by the old man's mood of the night before.

Things seemed to be back to normal, whatever normal was in this neck of the woods. He got up to refresh his coffee and in that moment he made a decision: he would keep the colt an entire - at least until his neck and chest had filled out and his true nature had come to the fore. So the colt would keep his valued testicles, for now, anyway. The die had been cast, he would be a prince for at least 18 months. Let's see what the old horse thinks of that, he chuckled to himself.

With the wild dog pack gone and the fire over with, except for the odd, still smoking big old round stumps, and the small flood having receded, the grass was up and growing healthily and the feed was rich and abundant.

The 'roo's had returned, as had the Pretty Face and Rock wallabies. They were all back as if nothing had happened. The voles and other furry little critters seemed to have come from nowhere and the bloody brown snakes and the red and yellow backs had taken up residence on the edge of the tree line, often venturing down across the fields hunting as many mice as they could find; filling themselves up for the autumn months ahead. The spiders were back in force and the old man had noticed not just red backs but some of the nasty so-called Sydney funnel webs happily in residence in the log piles that had survived the fire's onslaught.

And yes, he had enough timber to last probably five years, all piled up where the bush fire brigade had left it after cutting their fire breaks. Luckily there was enough tucker for all the predatory livestock around the place for the snakes not to invade the sanctuary of the barn. The guinea fowl and peacocks and their hens were still parading about the place, his veggie garden was bursting at the seams and the colt was working extraordinarily well in the round yard. He now carried a stock saddle on his back as if it had always been there.

Life was OK, the doctor had given him as clean a bill of health as someone with stuffed up lungs and a wrecked back could hope for and with the help of moderate painkillers he was surviving quite well. His doctor had mentioned that only a couple of brandies a week would be a better idea for his heart than two or three after dinner. That was not too hard to cope with as the red wine still flowed and the Bloody Mary's were a respectable colour and not as he had often said of the late Patrick Wymark's, you could hardly tell that a tomato had been anywhere near the vodka.

There were times when he really missed old mates from an era long ago. The farm was not quite the same as it used to be with the hustle and bustle that sprang from running different types of cattle and his beloved horses.

Thc vcranda was as inviting as ever with its huge stand of Datura in the eastern corner. He loved the smell that came from the white and yellow trumpets that in the wrong context could be used as a hallucinogenic. The rhododendrons were out in force and the large elk and stag horns were doing well on the sheltered side of the house.

It meant that walking up the steps to the veranda proper was a sheer delight as the blues or jazz or any of a number of forms of music would be playing. Having been through the sixties and seventies in busy London, New York and the French Riviera, his taste in music was vast and at times quite explosive. Thank God for *BB King* and the *Rolling Stones* early years, *Bob Dylan, Bert Jansch* and *John Renbourn; Queen*, the list goes on and on, with *Cher* dancing on that navel gun boat wearing very little and appealing to all. And *Good Morning Vietnam*, how *Robin Williams* was missed, how many other greats had gone …*Mama Cass*… not in this man's world, anyway, from the obscure to the obvious their music was all here and if it wasn't it would be found on the internet.

"Another day, another thirty-three cents mate, you sleep-ing?"

"Oh, hey, good morning Trevor, you're a week early."

"Shit, mate does that mean you gotta defrost the steak, if so, get to it quick, smart little buddy."

"Now when would I ever have to do that," said the old man, "they are sitting in the fridge and aged beautifully," he winked and smiled.

"Cool and groovy, as you would say old mate, so, let's have a look at the colt, eh, and see how his feet are doing. And then the old horse and mate, then the bloody breakfast - have I got an appetite or what? And a small surprise, but that you will have to wait for. Come on mate, can't hang about too long, gotta make a dollar to pay the tax man."

"Your script never changes," said the old man under his breath. He was probably one of the very few people who knew what Trevor was worth and it was a tidy old sum at that. "Pay the bloody tax man, who are you kidding?"

"Oi, Oi, we are the most watched and scrutinised race on the planet, the bloody satellites have got us all marked mate, so when I say loudly gotta pay the tax man, just bloody nod and agree with me, alright?"

Trevor was with the colt and said, "Has he been going round evenly, or a bit more to the right?"

"Why do you ask?"

"Well, his shoes are worn unevenly - just wondering if it's a weight shift or down to you sending him round to the right for longer periods."

"No, Trevor, I've been keeping him at even circles."

"Right, let's have a look at his pasterns and knee joints. He seems fine, I think he must be pushing harder to one side, he should even out. I'll have a look in four weeks, just keep our eye on it."

"Cool, will do."

"Right, let's look at the old stallion."

They moved next door and the stallion nickered as they came into his stable. And seeing Trevor he lifted one front leg and just held it up, waiting for the farrier to grasp it and cradle the hoof, putting the claw of his hammer into the gap between hoof and shoe. It was off before you could blink and then Trevor was working away with his paring knife with all the confidence in the world.

He knew the old horse's feet so well, as he did most of the horses that he worked on. So any imperfection was quickly addressed and sorted out with more than competent hands.

The hoof was done and he put it down, stretched his back out and picked up the packet of shoes brought especially for this particular horse. Before you could blink the hoof was back in his hands and the first nail was in and firmly attached; the other five nails followed and he was on to the hind leg on the same side, which the old horse had lifted up the minute that the front one was on the ground.

"I wish they all had his manners," said Trevor.

It hadn't always been like this when the stallion was young, they had to tie his feet up to teach him a little respect. When you worked with livestock you were always learning as no two animals were ever the same and being animals, they react with great speed and if you are in the way it can be a very painful experience. The last shoe was on and the two men left the stallion's stable.

Trevor put his gear in the back of the Tojo, his old dog chained in the back guarding the shoeing gear as always, very quietly with an all-seeing eye on everything around her. Trevor always had bitches; he had a thing about dogs, he would train them but refrain from keeping one, something about loyalty and lust, and he reckoned that the latter always won with a dog, whereas a bitch would stay with you till the end. Probably right in most cases, then again there was always the exception to the rule.

The veranda steps were negotiated and the cast iron skillet was on the combustion stove and the coffee poured within seconds, as the two old men sat down to talk before the mandatory breakfast was on the plates. Then there would be complete silence - why would you even think to interrupt a fine steak with idle chatter.

"The red dog was a bit of a loss, then again…"

"I know, Trevor, shit happens."

"And ain't that the truth," said Trevor as he looked towards the stove, "Smells about right for the eggs to go on, mate."

A flip of the slice and the plates were on the table, and the pepper was being ground onto the raw tomatoes. Silence reigned which for the old man was good, as he didn't really want to discuss the red dog anymore, he had enough with his own thoughts without anyone else's opinions and so it was that the ritual of breakfast was once again played out.

As the plates were removed and the coffee replenished they looked at each other and the old man said,

"if they knew how good they tasted they'd never come anywhere near us or a yard."

"Can't beat good home grown beef," said Trevor, "Well, gotta go, gotta make a dollar to pay, I know old mate it's always the same, even though the tax man never sees it you gotta make it." They both laughed.

"Oh, I stopped at the barn on the way up, you might like to check it out, I wouldn't leave it too long," and he winked, slammed the truck door shut, grated the gears and with the obligatory song drove out of the yard and away into the mid-morning light.

"Another shoeing done, another breakfast eaten and another day well on its way… The barn, I wonder what the old bugger has left there, ah, well, if I don't look I will never know." And he strode off with the wall-eyed dog close on his heel.

TWENTY-ONE
A Newcomer

The old man walked past the stallion's yard and tried not to let his eyes wander across to the mound in the middle of the slab wall. Eventually it would be a white rose bush and a happy memory but right now it was a rather raw wound.

He entered the barn and looked around, nothing really stood out, what on earth had Trevor done? Then all of a sudden the wall-eyed dog gave a small growl and was looking at an old potato sack that was over by one of the big round barn supports. There was an addition to the sack that was out of the ordinary, something that had very pointed ears, brown and white and standing up like radio antennas and far too big for the little body that emerged from under the sack. It had long legs and a pointed nose and a long tail. Nothing seemed to go together - what a mish-mash.

It cocked its head sideways and lifted one leg to scratch itself behind a long pointed ear and fell over. The wall-eyed dog went over very slowly to this strange looking puppy and reached out her nose to sniff it. The pup responded with a curled tongue that flashed out and caught Squint by surprise as it licked her nose. It showed no fear at all. Its tail wagged and it sat down. It looked absolutely ridiculous with its upright ears and its long skinny tail.

The old man walked over to it and picked it up by its tail and it hung there upside down not making a sound. Some of the old boys said you could tell the mettle of a dog this way; because if it squealed it was no damn good but if it kept quiet it was worth a try out. There was not one sound, it just hung there. It was then that he noticed there were two ruddy balls, heaven help us, Trev had left a male puppy! Not relinquishing his hold on the pup's tail he made his way back to the house; setting him upright, he clipped the pup to the veranda wall. He went inside and poured himself a cup of coffee and sat down to ruminate on this new arrival and what he would say to his farrier later on the phone.

The conversation that night was more about the colt than the strange-looking puppy, though he did ascertain that the dog was out of a prize winning working kelpie by a Queensland blue cross dingo; that would explain the ears. The kelpie side would contribute to the legs, and the body - well, that was anyone's guess. Maybe he would grow into all the bits that at the moment did not seem in any way related. He looked like he had been put together by someone who had no idea what they were doing. Except that they must have had a great sense of humour. Ah, well, better give him some grub and a blanket of his own to curl up on. Mustn't get too attached, as he might not make the grade, plus he was not looking for another dog and especially not a male. Trevor had stressed one point, which was that if he was looking for a dog himself then he would not have looked past this one; he would have kept him as he considered that he would make a fine dog after he had become a whole dog and not a jigsaw puzzle.

Trev said, "You just watch that pup come together; he has the makings of a very bright animal and would be an asset to have around."

That was something that would be interesting to see because at the moment he didn't look much of anything at all.

The old man went out onto the veranda carrying a bowl of food and was, to say the least, surprised at what confronted him. There were two long pointed ears sticking up between two curled up ginger cats. The bookends had wound themselves around the pup and were to all intents and purposes fast asleep, purring loudly. They had adopted the new arrival and were making it quite clear that he was part of the family. He put a dish down next to the bundle of fur with ears in the middle that now looked like some strange space creature. He went back inside, collected a coffee and returned to the veranda, sitting at the table he watched the pulsating, purring collective in the corner, and then smiled. It was that look, the one that said it all, the dog was staying; he was at home, the bookends had made the decision for him. Their approval of the new arrival had been noted and he sipped his coffee and looked out over the yard, taking in the stables, the entrance to the barn and the new mound of earth by the slabs on the lean to. He looked down at the wall-eyed dog lying peacefully next to his chair then sighed deeply, put his feet on the handrail and closed his eyes. Rugged up and protected from the slight evening breeze, he let his mind wander as the cats purred and Squint breathed noisily. The odd moth circled the lights on the veranda wall and one of the horses below stamped their hoof on the stable floor, and there was peace at the farm.

It was about a week or so later that the old man realised that the new addition had yet not barked. Not even a small yip; quite strange, he thought as he watched him curl himself into a ball, putting his nose under his tail for added warmth. The bookends had spent time with him every day, lying next to or on him as they chose. He never once complained; the three of them greeted each other with the cats rubbing the whole length of their bodies against his, bashing their heads into him in their way of showing affection and waving their tails about like sail cloth in the wind, only to settle down snuggled up like gloves and a cap thrown onto a hall seat.

This sort of morning ritual was not unusual for the bookends, they had done it for as long as he could remember with the now departed red dog. Never ever with Squint, even though they were friends, they didn't seem to have that closeness that prevailed with the Fox and with this new pup. The bookends would be in the barn early and then come back up to the house for their morning milk, curling up for an hour or so and then would begin another leisurely day; they would stretch, groom, and then set off for wherever they felt like, an ideal way of life if you were a cat.

"Come on, pup, let's see how you get on with the horses."

The old man clipped the lead onto the pup and the other end to his belt. This way, wherever he went the pup had no choice but to follow. It also meant that both hands were free to do whatever he needed to and there was none of that tugging stuff that you so often see with town dogs, they seem to spend their lives being pulled here, there and everywhere.

This way the dog was always at his heel and that just seemed to be the right place to be, right from the beginning. When he was mounted and the dog was running free, he would have a pocket full of little pebbles and when the dog went in front of the horse without being told to he would aim a tiny stone at his hind quarters, at the same time calling out, 'Come behind' and the pup would soon realise that was the safest place to be.

And that was how he taught all his dogs to heel to the horse, whether it was the right way according to other people's opinion, didn't really matter because it worked for him. And unlike some people who gave their dogs a quick flick of the whip to bring them back, he preferred his method. He used the whip either by cracking it to get their attention, or to stop them barking at night, but never to actually hit the dog. He never forced his way onto others; his way of thinking was to learn by observing, not by being told.

The pup was a bit wary of the large animals in their stables and kept very, very close to the old man's heels. Never taking his eyes off the horses, when the stallion put his nose down to smell the new pup he held his ground with just a small curl of his lip at which the horse blew out through his nose covering the pup in globules of moisture, making him shake vigorously. But he never made a move backwards, just stood his ground and waited to see what would happen next.

The horse then ignored him and turning his attention to the old man, put his head on the man's shoulder, fiddling with the collar of his jacket with his lips and getting hold of it with his teeth and pulling ever so gently, twitching his nose at the same time, eyes closed, apparently in seventh heaven just at the fact that he was in close contact with his friend.

TWENTY-TWO
A Line is Crossed

The dog pack had made themselves at home six valleys away and had collected more females from local farms and strays that had been dumped and had found their way there too. The new yet now totally in charge pig-dog-come-lurcher, being the lead bitch's undisputed mate, had dispensed any new male dogs that had appeared on the scene and was a formidable adversary. He would remain so until he was ousted by another dog and being in his prime that would not happen in the foreseeable future.

This was indeed a pack to be reckoned with, well structured, with territory well enforced, and as this covered such a large portion of ground, their home base had not as yet been discovered. Their assault on the local livestock had not been put down to one pack, more to wandering dogs or dingoes on the move. The pack had successfully taken control of more than nine valleys and all the hillsides. The local indigenous game was so plentiful that their minor forays into the areas with new calves, and the sheep populations, was hardly a matter for concern.

The packs' lives could be classed as Utopian, and nothing in the immediate future looked as if it would change that. The lead couple had a litter of pups and all seven had survived and were now running with the main pack. Only six months old, they were becoming quite a force in their own right: five bitches and two dogs all of them favouring their father in size and in temperament. They ran together as a mini pack, always directly behind their parents and sometimes spread out in a line as if to stop any other dogs coming between them and the dog and bitch that gave them life.

Their presence was beginning to be felt by the rest of the pack. They might still be quite young, but they were united and all stood together; attack or threaten one and you had to deal with them all. It was this simple fact that would have repercussions for the whole pack in the not too distant future.

The old man and his mate, who was a stock and station agent as well as an auctioneer, were out mustering cattle in one of the valleys that lay within the dog packs' terrain. The hillsides and the top ridges had to be covered because they usually held quite a few of the adventurous cattle looking for mountain grazing and peace and quiet, as the usual mustering never ventured onto the higher ledges. But on the big musters it was a different matter and the old man often accompanied his friend on these excursions.

They had between them six dogs, two being Squint and the new pup who was now between nine and twelve months old. They were on top of one of the higher ridges when on rounding a corner they were greeted with the sight of the seven young crossbreeds lying in the middle of the path, tongues hanging out from their recent hunt. The rest of the pack had melted into the surrounding bush but the youngsters had just flopped down where they stood. They were apparently oblivious to the men and their horses and dogs. At the sight of this collection rounding the bend, some of them sat, but most of them stood up and their growling was not to be ignored or taken lightly.

"Holy shit old man, call your dogs between the horses and get your stock whip ready, this could get a bit nasty. And stay abreast of me - we don't want to give them a chance of getting to the dogs. Just keep moving at the same pace." His dogs were all males but they had all been cut bar one.

"That big feller of mine will let us know if any dogs come up behind - he is very cluey when it comes to dingoes and wild packs.

"Now get that young gun of yours in quick smart, they will pick him off first, they are quite young but look at the bloody size of them."

The dogs had started to grow their winter coats and it gave them the appearance of very large wolves. This united pack of brothers and sisters showed no inclination to flee; instead they just stood there in the middle of the track, heads outstretched and lips drawn back showing clean white teeth and no fear at all.

The stallion was already sweating profusely and dancing on the spot; he had smelt the pack and his memories were not good. His ears were pinned back and he was gnashing his teeth against the bit, his neck was arched and he looked to all intents and purposes ready for battle. The old man could feel his back starting to arch and curve outwards, this usually preceded an enormous buck and then flailing front feet smashing into anything in front of him. The old man sat deep in the saddle and said very firmly, "Settle old lad, settle." The stallion responded by lessening the arch but his blood was running hot and he wanted to fight, his hind quarters were bunched under him like a spring ready to uncoil at any moment.

The old man had unfurled his stock whip and had not taken his eyes off the dogs ahead of them. They had not taken a step backwards, if anything they had edged forwards a fraction and looked ready to hurl themselves directly at them at the drop of a hat.

"Aim to cut them nose and arse; get them confused as to where they are being attacked from. Open 'em up old mate, we only have one chance of getting out of this. These dogs don't give a shit and we have a big problem; stay level with me to protect our dogs as much as we can and let's get up these buggers. Ready, right, let's do it and as much noise as you can muster. Go! Now!"

And they both released their mounts and headed straight into the young pack, whips cracking and laying into the wild dogs as best they could. Agile wasn't the word; the dogs were everywhere at once, avoiding the tail end of the whips and trying to get at the working dogs, making short dashes at the horses' legs.

The stallion was enraged and was kicking out hard and fast, the old man just sat deep and let the horse have as much of his head as it was safe to do. They must have looked like mounted aggressors at a bull fight, their dogs keeping between the horses' feet, staying out of the battle around them. They were obviously confused as they were being told continuously to come in and stay.

The whip ends were having some effect as they opened up long welts on the muzzles, heads and hind quarters of the young pack. Blood was starting to flow and the dogs were shaking their heads and spinning around as the whips made contact with their arses. One of the bitches made a break for the scrub and another followed, the two horses thundered on, whips cracked and the old man and his mate were shouting obscenities at the pack. They had them on the back foot now and they were not going to let their advantage go.

They went through the pack and the stallion let go a hind leg and from the whelping sound that ensued it was clear he had made contact with one of the wild dogs and left his mark imprinted on the dog's flank. Suddenly they were through the dogs and when they looked back the track was empty. The dogs had blended with the bush and become invisible.

"Keep going, old mate," said stockman, "Let's get the hell out of here and down to the flats," and off they went at a very sharp pace indeed, their dogs went ahead sending up puffs of dirt as their paws hit the dry ground. And the horses followed, leaving behind an even bigger trail of dust and dirt. They didn't stop until they reached the river that wended its way along the valley floor. The dogs threw themselves into the water, panting, gasping and drinking all at the same time. The horses put their noses in the water and drank deep and hard.

The stockman looked at the old man, a bit of a grin on his face as he said matter-of-factly,

"Well, old mate, now we know where the buggers are we had better get the word out, 'cause they certainly don't have any fear of men. That was a bit of an adrenalin rush - what do you reckon?"

"We were lucky mate, we were lucky. If that had been a couple of young guns out for a ride with their dogs, they wouldn't have stood a chance. By the look of those dogs back there I would take a guess and say that the old bitch had joined up with that pigging dog that went missing early last spring, and they were her first litter to him, which means she'll be about due to drop another lot real soon. You're right, they have got to go, we had better get some of the boys together and get into them quick smart before they hurt someone. It's a good excuse to go to the hotel and put a schooner away, what do you reckon?"

"Suits me," said the stockman and they called up their dogs who were now just lying in the shallow water, cooling off and they made their way back to the truck and to the hotel.

Back on the ridge the young dogs were licking their wounds. Some of them had caught the whip across their muzzles and one had been opened up to the bone. Some were bleeding from mainly superficial cuts and most of them carried cuts on the hindquarters. The dog that the stallion had kicked was limping quite badly as her shoulder had caught the full force of the kick, but luckily for her it had not broken; it would stiffen up later after she had snoozed and recuperated from the morning's frenzy.

They had no idea that their lack of wisdom would bring down retribution on the whole pack. If only they had followed their elders and left the track instead of behaving like young hooligans in a car park, they could have enjoyed comparative freedom for as long as they liked. Now their time was limited because there was no way that wild dogs or dingoes who attacked a man would be allowed to live. War was about to be declared.

It was about a week later and the old man was sitting in his favourite chair with the log fire blazing away when he heard a long, drawn out howl. He left his chair with speed and he turned on the outside lights and opened the door in one fluid movement. The thought that immediately crossed his mind was that the dog pack was back.

His shock was paramount as the halogen lights lit up the yard and there was his nearly one year old pup sitting in the middle of the yard with his head thrown back at an angle that pointed directly at the moon. His neck full of air and his mouth barely open, he was howling at the sky. This was the very first time the old man had heard one sound come out of the pup except for an occasional growl, never a bark and most certainly never a howl. And yet here he was, proclaiming his stature to the world. The old man called out to him,

"Oi, Pavarotti, what the devil is all this noise about?"

And that is how he got his name; Pavarotti it was, and Pav for short. Out mustering one day he called the pup back to him and his mate said,

"Pav a bloody what? You can't call a dog that, what's wrong with Jess or Blackie or Ted or anything except Pav-a-bloody-rotti."

"He sings," said the old man, and that was that.

"Bloody snapping duck shit, I never heard anything so bloody stupid in my life, Pav-a-bloody-rotti."

"Mate, you can call 'em what you like as long as they get the job done and just look at him work."

"Not denying that, it's the bloody name you've given him; he will be the laughing stock of every fire."

"It won't bother him," said the old man and he put a little pressure on the stallion and they jumped forward to join his pup.

Most nights when the moon was up, you would hear him howl, long, lingering, mournful and soulful all at the same time. And the old man would sit in his chair and smile to himself as his dog with ears too big and legs too long howled at the moon. And the fire crackled and spat out tiny sparks as the gases held in the logs was freed, and the bookends sprawled across the back of his chair and Squint lay in front of the fire as the old man flicked an ember off her fur. Life was cool and groovy if you just let it unfurl in its own way. The dog howled, the cats purred the stallion stamped his foot and made his night a contented and peaceful experience.

TWENTY-THREE
A Battle Royale

The next morning saw the stallion back in his day yard and the colt with the saddle and bridle on him and the old man getting on and off from either side, as you never knew when you would be in a situation where mounting from the nearside was impossible. He was - dare to say it - very impressed with the way the colt had come on. It would appear that he not only had a brain, but also had a fair amount of common sense, not always an attribute carried by the Arabian breed.

His capacity for learning was a joy. Now, having got over the initial shock of being hunted and driven around the place, he had settled down and seemed genuinely interested in what to do next. He accepted the saddle and bridle without too much fuss and was not overly perturbed by the old man's weight on his back. The bit, which was a very kind snaffle, had become something he seemed to enjoy playing with once in his mouth. He had understandably played up a little when introduced to the crupper but he soon lost interest in the fact that there was something between the top end of his tail and his back end. He just lifted up his tail and was quite happy to have the piece of leather, which was covered in cream so as not to rub, placed in its correct position. The pressure it put on him when going downhill to prevent the saddle moving forwards did not seem to bother him at all, in fact it looked as if he was going to make a great mount with a kind disposition. This did not detract from the fact that he was a spirited and very handsome young boy with amazing carriage and presence. He was a dead ringer for his sire and that was a compliment indeed.

He put the colt in his own day yard and looked at the stallion. Why not, he mused to himself, and so saying, he got the stallion's head collar from the tack room and hung it over his shoulder. Putting the head collar on the stallion he then attached a lead rope and entered the round yard. Unclipping the lead rope he stroked the horse's head and neck and then said,

"Out, get out, boy," the stallion moved to the outside of the circle and stood waiting for the next command.

He stood there while the old man rolled a thin single paper cigarette. He didn't light it, he just held it in his fingers and said,

"Walk on," the stallion turned side on and walked off.

After three laps of the round yard the old man said,

"Stretch out," and the horse extended his stride.

Next came the command,

"Trot on," and he did, "Hup," and the horse trotted out.

The old man clicked his tongue and the horse threw his legs out in front of him stretching so far out that he looked as if he was floating on air. The old man smiled and clicked his tongue again and the stallion started a slow collected canter, head arched, neck bent, hind quarters tucked up underneath his belly, totally controlled, and he shook his head and snorted,

"Alright, get on with you," and the horse gathered himself up and extending his stride threw himself forwards and galloped around the yard, the old man laughed as the horse bucked and squealed in sheer joy.

Maybe, just one more ride; the horse was certainly fit enough and he was still an open horse so he could do a gentle 80 kilometre ride; a 40km in four hours, a vet check and another 40km. Why not? Then that was settled; he spent another twenty minutes working the stallion, who did not even break a sweat.

He took him over to the wash bay and hosed him down with warm, but not hot water. He scraped the excess water off and walked the stallion for about fifteen minutes before placing him in his yard with a very light day rug just to keep the possibility of a slight chill at bay. The stallion bucked, snorted, farted and then put his head down to enjoy the biscuit of Lucerne that the old man had put in his yard. Joy of joys as the fine stalks tickled his nose and his whole body relaxed; his head drooped, his eyes rolled and his lips twitched; he was in horse heaven.

The old man laughed quietly to himself and walked over to the tack room. Today was clean saddles day and the smell of the leather as he covered it in soap and then a rich cream, was something he would never tire of. The bits were hanging in a bucket of lukewarm water; it didn't matter if they had not been used recently they all got the same treatment on cleaning day. Everything had to be the most comfortable for its recipient. He rolled another cigarette as the one from the round yard had disintegrated. He lit it with his old square Dunhill lighter and as he watched the tiny plume of smoke head up towards the rafters he thought, what a stupid habit this is; a complete waste of money apart from anything else, and he had to admit his chest was feeling a little tight today; he had not really noticed this before. Then again maybe he had and had just ignored it.

Never mind, back to giving the tack its once over, and the day passed with him surrounded by smells he loved and sounds that made him happy. The wall-eyed dog was sitting at his feet and Pavarotti was just outside the tack room door, stretched out in the afternoon sun.

He remembered the first time he had taken him to Surfers Paradise to see George and guard the car. Usually he would take the truck, if only to give it a run, but this day he decided to take the Escort. The engine had been rebored and when necessary she flew along at a rate of knots.

Having arrived at Surfers he had left Pavarotti with strict instructions to guard the car. He left two windows open slightly and took off with his mate for a late supper and a visit to the clubs. It was not a regular practice for the old man but when he did join George for an out and about night in the clubs they never had to pay for their drinks, they were all supplied by the management.

On this occasion he only had a couple of Millers as he was going to drive home around the 5.00 am mark. They approached the little Escort before five and George had started to laugh long before they reached the car. The old man looked at him, shaking his head,

"What on earth has got you going?"

"Wait and see," said George between what was now spasmodic hilarity. Pavarotti was standing up wagging his tail with such vigour that his whole body looked like it would take off.

"Notice anything strange?" said George.

The old man looked and was suddenly aware that all was not well. The seats were down to their metal frames and the roof lining no longer existed; the inside of the car was a total right-off. He let Pavarotti out, who went to the nearest wall and lifted his leg. When finished he jumped back into the car sitting precariously on the metal frame of the passenger seat.

"Have a great trip home, old mate," and George left very quickly laughing his head off. "I'll call you," he shouted back over his shoulder and disappeared into the stately apartment block that housed his penthouse.

The old man got into what was left of the car's interior, and revving the car just enough to get the oil going around the engine put it in first gear and started the journey home in silence.

Looking out of the windscreen at the coming dawn, he wondered why on earth the dog had destroyed the inside of the car. Pavarotti half sitting, half standing, looked through the windscreen with totally different thoughts. When they got home he let Pavarotti run around for fifteen minutes before putting him on a chain, then proceeded to the kitchen to get a well-deserved coffee and to contemplate the night's happenings.

As he sat on the veranda with his coffee in his hand he started to chuckle - what on earth had prompted the dog to rip the little car to bits? People teasing him perhaps, Surfers' Paradise was full of drunken young teenagers walking round the place with nothing better to do than be a total disgrace to themselves and their parents. He had given up cities and what used to be exciting times, mainly because of the habits of today's youth: the stealing, destruction of property and indiscriminate fighting, usually more than two or three against some unsuspecting person who had no idea how cowards made themselves feel important - by bashing some innocent for fun.

"Ah, well, I suppose I better check out the damage to the car," he rose and walked to the small barn where he kept his motors, throwing a biscuit of Lucerne into the colt's stable and one into the stallion's. They could eat them before he put them into their day yards with their hard feed.

Looking at the interior of the once proud little Escort was quite a shock; on closer inspection Pavarotti had done a demolition job that any destructive person would have been proud of. So the old man got a dustpan and brush. He had contemplated opening the doors and just letting the high pressure hose vent its anger but decided against what could have been fun. He started the arduous task of cleaning out from under the seats. As he pulled out the bits and pieces of seating that were wedged under the front passenger seat he was suddenly confronted by a very mangled piece of congealed bloody meat. He looked at it closely and was amazed to find that it was the chewed up head of a carpet snake and not too small a one at that. As he kept cleaning he came across the rest of the snake - about six to eight feet of very chewed and mangled up python.

Then it all became clear: it would appear that the snake had curled itself up in the car and fallen asleep. It had woken up at some time or another and taken umbrage at the other passenger - namely Pavarotti. It would appear that the snake had thrown a coil around the dog's body, trying to apply pressure as only a python can. Pavarotti had fought back with a vengeance. The snake's body was torn to pieces probably after it was dead. How Pavarotti must have fought and how much vengeance he had taken out on the car's interior: a battle royal indeed. The old man looked at the dog with a revised respect and the damage to the car's interior was instantly forgotten. Pavarotti's desire to survive was extremely courageous - obviously not a spirit to be tangled with as an aggressor.

The old man continued with his leather cleaning and both dogs stretched out for completely different reasons as the day progressed.

TWENTY-FOUR
Retribution

It was the gears grinding and grunting of the truck engine that got the bitch's attention and she wandered over to the outside edge of the dogs' hilltop lair to look down onto the valley floor to see what the noisy intrusion was. She watched with interest as the two trucks, one big, one small, made their way along the dirt road that wound along the valley.

She didn't differentiate between them, they were just two noisy things that came and went, usually meaning the arrival of men, horses and dogs. A half-hearted attempt at scratching her ear with a hind foot missed, so the paw struck the ground and clipped a piece of sharp rock, making her squeak slightly. This caught her mate's attention and after stretching he sauntered over to her and lifting his leg urinated on a hardy looking fern, while at the same time watching half-heartedly as the truck with the four by four behind it towing its float ground its way up the valley floor below.

It wasn't what you would call an arduous haul, yet it was a steady climb to the first ledge where they could unload and turn around before parking. This would be their base camp for as long as the exercise of pack scattering and removal lasted. It was a cool but not overly cold Thursday morning, and by now there were at least twelve of the feral dogs watching as the horses were unloaded from their transport. The horses skittered down the ramp and spun around their owners to avoid having their bits jag at their mouths. The one thing you could never accuse these work horses of being, was stupid, when it came to a lesson hard learned. Some of the old Cow Cockies were not the lightest in the hands-on department, and the stock soon learned what was what.

The difference between the old man and some of his cohorts was noticeable; the stallion waited till the ramp was down and he heard the old man say, "Back up, old son," and that was exactly what he did. No rush, just one foot after the other till terra firma had been reached, then a quick stretch and a shake and he was ready to go and do whatever was asked of him. He looked around at the other horses and gave a half-hearted whinny just to let them all know that he was here, in case they hadn't realised there was an entire present. "Settle down," said his friend, giving him a pat on the neck, and a carrot suddenly appeared from his pocket. As soon as they set off there would be reddish foam gathered around the stallion's mouth as he relished his treat and consequently frothed up. Then he would shake his head sending little bits of carrot out into the morning air.

The old man swung his leg over the stallion's rump and double checked that the rifle was securely sitting in its leather sheath. This done, he headed towards the men who were milling round, getting their girths tightened and other little tweaks that they needed to do before setting off on what could be quite a tough, rough old ride.

Working on mountain slopes always had its dangers, loose footing, buried bits of tree trunk that poked up out of nowhere, usually covered in moss and other flora, disguising its dangers as it caused a trip or a fall. Even just a small stumble could quite easily unseat a too relaxed rider, there again there was always the trapped leg and badly bruised or even torn tendon.

No, working the mountain could never be classed as easy, especially when chasing run away cattle or in this case getting up the wild dogs and giving them as hard a time as one possibly could, shooting as many as possible with clean shots. Even though they were cruel, and classed as vermin and did the most awful damage to calves and sheep, to have them suffer was of no advantage at all. A good clean shot and on to the next one; they were here for a purpose, getting rid of or scattering the pack, as big a cull as possible.

Now that everyone was girthed up and hats pulled down over foreheads, feet jammed into their stirrups, no laughter or big smiles, this was a work day that nobody really enjoyed. It was kill and scatter and try very hard not to come off and break anything. "Right, boys, let's get at 'um." And they peeled off across and up the mountain, looking for sign. The hard riding was yet to come.

By now most of the dog pack were gathered at the edge of the ledge and were watching the horses and riders below. It seemed strange to them that there were no dogs, just the men, some of them had the sticks that barked that would send a dog reeling backwards never to run again. All the men had them, some were attached to their horses while others had them across their laps. The pack was becoming uneasy, this did not seem to be the usual coming and going of man; no dogs, no joking or banter between the men, they just rode onward and upward looking all the time at the ground and occasionally with a hand shielding their eyes from the bright morning sun.

The lead bitch growled and started to move off and her nearly full grown pups followed her, with the rest of the pack behind - a tightly bunched collection of cross breed dogs that had become a menace to all who lived within a 50-mile radius of their den.

Instead of climbing up in a straight line, the dogs traversed the mountain from side to side, taking advantage of every little wallaby track or dry water course that criss-crossed the now steepening terrain. It saved their muscles and was easier on the lungs. To go in a straight line would have put a strain on their hindquarters, and tired them much sooner.

The men had reached the ledge and were giving their horses a well-earned rest. At the same time they were assessing the strength of thc pack. It would appear that the pack had been using the ledge for quite a while as there was a lot of sign here, including carcasses of kill: more wallabies and 'roos than calves and sheep - and a few wild goat remains scattered the edges of the den. It had all the appearances of a well-used den of about thirty or so dogs. This was a substantial collection of preying adversaries whose diet included everything that man relied on as a cash crop - cattle, sheep or commercial goat herds - and the chickens, ducks and other fowl that man might raise for eggs or meat for their personal survival. Not forgetting the kids' pets; if it was edible, they killed it, simple as that, survival meant destruction.

The dogs had reached the next small plateau and they stopped to have a slight rest and a drink from the small pool of water that sat at the base of the rocky incline still to be climbed before they reached the very top. Once there, they could navigate their way along the flat ridge to any number of exits to the valleys below. There was abundant water from the springs that started at the top of the mountain; no one really knew where they came from, but blue dye had been put in a water source in Papua New Guinea and one of the springs up here had suddenly come out blue - to explain that would be geologists' joy, the farmers didn't know how water from PNG found its way up here, so the mystery remains for another day.

Refreshed and ready to go the dog pack moved off on the last leg of their hill climb. Below them and about fifteen minutes behind, the horses were making good headway, even though some of them were blowing slightly. On reaching the ridge that the dogs had just left, their presence was evident and the men knew how long it had been before they left by the small amounts of water left in their tracks by the water hole.

The old man was happy with the way the stallion was travelling, his breathing was steady and he was as fresh as when he started the climb. If nothing else he was giving the impression of being ride fit, meaning that he so far looked as if he could easily do a 40 kilometre ride. The horses greedily sucked up the spring water and shook themselves vigorously as if trying very hard to get rid of their saddles, having adjusted girths and slightly slipped saddles. All that could be heard was the clinking of bits and the stamping of shod hooves. The horses were ready to start the last leg of the strenuous climb. Then as if on cue they all moved off in unison; the atmosphere had suddenly changed, it was really serious now, the hunt was on.

The dogs were now on the top ridge and without taking a breather had moved on at a steady lope, they could keep this up for hours and cover 50 miles in one day with ease. This equated to 80 kilometres and was a feat indeed as they could do it day after day. With their tongues out swelling and slavering they avoided overheating; the only way a dog can sweat to cool down is through its pads or by lolling out its tongue. Any spring or surface water would be eagerly lapped up or lain in to help adjust their temperature. It was much colder here on the top of the mountain and they were taking advantage of the freshness to even out any strain incurred on the steep climb up. So they were not panicking, even though they knew their adversaries were not far behind them. They knew that if they kept up their steady pace not only would they conserve energy, they would out-run their aggressors and tire them out long before they ran out of steam.

The riders arrived at the top ridge without too much drama. One of the horses had lost a shoe and one had pricked itself just above the coronet and had a small pulsating bleed. The lost shoe was overcome by putting a boot on; a lot of the riders carried these with them, and the bleed was addressed by tying a thin scarf above the bleed with just enough pressure to stop the flow. If caught in the bush without anything to tie around the leg, a strong blade of grass or dead weed could also do the trick. The Cow Cocky on the horse with the boot on rode with his mate on the horse with the bleed to keep him company. It would only take about half an hour for the bleed to congeal and then they could canter on at a slow even pace.

The others led by the old man had cantered off at a respectable speed; the old man's stallion, much to his joy, showed no stress from his climb and settled down to the job at hand. His breathing was steady and he had not even broken a sweat; this exercise would complete his training for the endurance ride and just lift his fitness up one more level. Even though this was not a great day as far as getting rid of the dog pack was concerned, it was serving as the best finish to the horse's fitness and the old man was secretly glowing inside. The stallion was as ready as he could have ever hoped to be for his (most likely) last ride ever competitively, which was shaping up to be one of the most memorable days of his life. The old man smiled inwardly and sat deep in the saddle to get on with the job.

The sign was so obvious that the men had no problem following the dogs; their prints were deeply set in the dirt. The dog with the injured shoulder was there, leaving her slightly uneven stride clearly visible to the trained eye. Out front, the lead dogs: the bitch could be identified quite clearly as she was heavy in pup and the prints were deeper than the others and her mate with his enormous pads left a splayed out footprint.

"They are travelling well," said the old man to Mark, who had ridden his stock horse upsides of the stallion. The two horses travelled abreast with no animosity at all; stallion and gelding with one agenda - to go wherever their masters asked them.

"They are well grouped," said Mark, "And I hate to say it, but they know exactly what they are doing, they are not trying to out-run us, they have set their pace and they are sticking to it.

There was a silence for a while and then the old man said,

"Mate, I think they will run the length of the ridge and go down close to the Queensland border. How are we going to play this, or do we just keep going and work it out later?"

"Well, having run them this far I am not going to lose them just because of the tick border, and that's for sure."

"I'm with you," said the old man and he put slight pressure onto the stallion's side asking him for a slight increase in pace.

Mark's horse responded; he was right there in tandem, the boys behind kept up and the pace was now on. The dogs would hear the increase if not by ear, then by the vibration in the ground. The game was on and it would not be long before it would be in earnest. How cunning would the pack be, and would the riders out-smart them?

The back markers had caught up with the horse with the bleed and the horse with the lost shoe was travelling well in the boot so the riders were back up to strength and all with one intent - no more bloody dogs.

The old man was still very happy with the stallion's condition; a couple of horses were blowing a bit harder than their riders would have liked but if necessary they would stop for a ten minute break and let them have a pick and a bit of a stroll; you would be amazed what a little snack and a small drink would do for a horse's equilibrium. Their recovery rate when they were as fit as this was something to behold, and they would catch up with the main group in no time at all.

As they all cantered on together, the stallion suddenly dropped his head and on bringing it back up his ears were flat to his skull and he snorted in disgust, as if he knew they were catching up and all he wanted was contact. His hatred for wild dogs was so ingrained that he burned with a sense of revenge deep inside him; woe betide any dog that got in his way. How he differentiated between the feral dogs and his friends at the farm was a mystery.

The dogs were loping along, necks stretched out, front feet hardly touching the ground, back legs and hind quarters pushing them onward with purpose. There was no panic, it was just steady; the older dogs were well aware that the horses had increased their pace and they had instinctively stepped up theirs.

The lead dogs knew that they would have to stop for some water. The bitch could smell it somewhere below them, how far she wasn't sure but it was there and she peeled off to the right and followed closely by the rest of the pack made her way down the steep side of the hill towards the sweet smelling scent. Her front legs lost themselves on the shale - only for a second - but that was enough to strain the muscles in her chest; hopefully she would work the pain out of them as she ran on. The water was in sight and the dogs picked up their pace.

The men were cantering along at a very respectable pace when from out of nowhere came a sound like no other. It was a scream of a dog in panic and pain.

"A trap," said Mark in a knowing sort of way.

"Nope, not a trap, mate," said the old man.

"What then?"

"Snake."

"Never."

"Snake," said the old man again, this time with a meaningful edge to his voice.

"Ten bucks it's a trap."

"Make it twenty and you got a bet,"

"Twenty it is."

"Snake," said the old man and they rode on.

It wasn't long before they came to where the tracks veered off to the right. All the horses had their ears pricked except the stallion, who still had his ears pinned back against his head. The other horses smelt the water and had to be held back as they tried hard to ride through the bit to get to the refreshing drink.

It was just as they neared the small spring fed dam that they came across the dog that had earlier screamed in pain and it was as the old man had guessed, the dog and snake were firmly attached in death. Concentrating on the enticing smell of water, the dog had let his attention slip. The death adder had been enjoying the mid-morning sun from the warmth of a rock and from nowhere came an intruder. The snake had flicked its body against the rock and launched itself towards the dog, who had seen it from the corner of its eye, spun and snapped. And so ended their lives; the dog had killed the snake, but not before the adder had filled her with its deadly venom.

The dog pack was down by one, and the old man was richer by twenty bucks. A good outcome, he thought quietly to himself. As the horses had not really broken a sweat and the day was not what one would call hot, it was safe for the horses to drink long and hard. They drank their fill and moved off slowly so that by the time they had got back onto the ridge it was no problem to canter off and keep on the trail of the dog pack. From the tracks left by the pack it was clear they were in no great hurry; just so long as they stayed ahead of their pursuers there did not seem to be any urgency.

To the men on horseback it was just another day in paradise, as the saying goes. The horses were well refreshed and eager to get on with the job in hand. Only the stallion seemed to know what the outcome of their trek must be and that was based on his hatred of the scent that filled his nostrils.

When riding in an endurance race, according to the purists, it was not a race; thus the saying, 'to complete is to win.' If you kept your mount within the trace odours of the mounts in front then your horse was seemingly dragged along by the scent of thc horses up ahead. And this was the case for the stallion now, he could smell the dog pack out in front and that seemed to stimulate his senses and make his journey less stressful. It was as if he was in a slip stream being dragged along with minimal effort on his part. He had one mindset and that was to find the dogs and administer his justice. The old man clicked to the stallion and he increased his pace, lengthening his stride, his front feet hitting the ground with a determination that to those who knew meant only one thing, he knew only one outcome and that was winning.

And so the chase continued and the outcome was not just in the lap of the gods, it was in the tracking, the lay of the land, the tenacity of the followers and the survival instincts of the dogs in front.

The dogs had veered off onto a small indistinct trail to the left of the main track. After traversing extremely difficult ground through valleys far into and past the Queensland border it led to the comparative safety of the rugged terrain that joined New South Wales and the Sunshine State. This was a no man's land of tall trees growing straight and towering over the nearly impenetrable Lantana, an invasive weed that had taken over areas of the Australian countryside and reached 8 to 10 feet high.

At ground level, it appeared as if someone had created a collection of tunnels joining many different areas together. It was not only wallabies and 'roos that had carved these passageways out of the noxious Lantana.

If you decided to enter one of these tunnels with a bit of width and height to it, then it was possible you might come across a solitary and quite angry Angus or Brangus bull. The

Hereford bull had an aversion to travelling up hill to forage and preferred the flats and the hay that arrived on a flat top truck. The tougher Brahman Angus cross was more likely to stray, as none of the cows in his paddocks were receptive to his advances. He had used his own tunnel system to travel to pastures green where there were cows of a different mind-set that accepted his pushy behaviour that inevitably ended in a rather rough and over-bearing mating. When he had exhausted the in-season collection of cows, he would once again become a solitary bull. As he was intent on avoiding the pervasive buffalo fly, he found relative safety in the Lantana passageways. Sometimes he would join up with another bull and together they would travel as bachelors on the prowl; but if the scent of a cow in season reached them they would instantly become their worst nightmare - bulls in lust intent on keeping the other from mating.

If the pack dogs could reach these tunnels that could take them to and from many a valley and keep them hidden from man, they would become as close to invincible as possible. This must not happen at any cost.

The men had upped the pace to the next notch plus one and were catching up and closing the gap between them and the dog pack. They were trotting and sometimes sliding down the narrow track when suddenly the rear of one of the last in line dogs came into view.

One of the men raised his rifle and the old man shouted, "Not yet," the man lowered his weapon with a questioning look.

Without missing a step, the old man said,

"If we fire now, they will scatter and run faster. If we wait then when they get to the bottom of the hill they will feel more secure and walk into the river that feeds the dam further down. If they do they'll be intent on drinking and cooling down. If we pick our targets and fire and re-aim we stand a chance of knocking out ten or twelve dogs before they start to wade to the shore. The water will slow them down and we could possibly knock out a few more.

"It's the old bull and young bull theory, where the young bull says to his grandad let's rush down and grab one and the old bull says let's saunter down and grab the lot. Well, now's our chance to see if it works. What do you reckon?"

There was a lot of nodding and a fair amount of grinning as the story-come-joke was refreshed in their memories.

"Good thinking, you old bastard, it's worth a shot, let's do it."

And so it was as they came to the tree line at the bottom of the hill. There they were… most of the dogs were immersed in the cooling waters of the gently flowing stream and those that weren't were standing in the water letting the ripples caress their underbellies, seemingly mesmerised by the action of the water against their bodies. After their arduous journey up, along and then down the mountain the dogs were in seventh heaven and unaware of the impending danger.

The men did not dismount, instead they steadied their mounts and quietly and with great concentration took aim. The stallion could hardly contain himself, yet knowing that to upset his old friend now would be more than his life was worth, he stood completely still and contained his anger. His turn would come, of that he had no doubt. The firing started and as the dogs became aware of the danger, the second round of fire filled the air and all that were still able came to life as one and seemed to lift themselves out of the water as if on wings. Their numbers were less than half of the original pack and the water slowed them down, and as another blast hit the air their numbers were reduced to a meagre five.

"Now," called out the old man and they all broke cover and galloped towards the river.

The dogs were taken completely by surprise and the two seconds of dithering was their final downfall. The big rangy pig dog was the first of the group to go; the bullet caught him high in the shoulder and he screamed and somersaulted sideways back into the water. The second shot caught him just behind the ear and that was the end of him.

The remaining younger pup with his big shaggy winter coat was the next casualty: a clean head shot and he dropped on the bank; the last remaining old dog sank below the surface as the bullet took his life with a heart shot.

This left only the lead bitch who had now turned towards her aggressors with bared teeth and stood her ground, her hind legs on dry land and her front just above the water line. She seemed to growl and howl in one haunting sound; the old man let the stallion go and without hesitation he had hurled himself into the water with one enormous leap and grabbed the dog by the scruff of her neck and was shaking her from side to side. The air was cut off and her neck was broken, but the stallion never let go; his being had reverted to nature and the true ferocious animal that lay beneath the surface came to the fore in unrelenting savagery.

His head was high in the air, the dog limp and not a vestige of life in its body; the stallion's neck was tight and solid as he was bent on the destruction of a memory that had come to the surface with a fury that had all who saw it spellbound. Then as quickly as it started it was over, and the dog was catapulted away. As the horse reached the bank he shook himself, seemingly getting rid of the last vestiges of hate. He took three paces then stopped and with a disdainful last look at the river, moved off only to stand quietly as if nothing had happened.

The other men looked on seemingly embarrassed at what they had witnessed. The old man stroked the stallion's neck and they moved off together. Only they knew why this had transpired; the stallion was now free of something that had plagued him for a long time and the old man felt the calm slowly overtake the stallion's body.

They started to count the dead bodies of the once feared dog pack. Things had happened today that would be the talk of many a drink session in someone's barn somewhere at the end of another mustering day. The riders left the bodies where they were. Between the goannas, the crows and various other birds, the wild pigs and the never-ending trail of ants, there would be nothing left to suggest that there had ever been a pack of wild dogs.

The pack would eventually be replaced by another pack - once again made up of dogs that had once been a loved puppy, but were now a nuisance to be got rid of. The effect that humans had on Mother Nature would never change, not in this old man's lifetime, anyway.

Once back at the old man's farm and their horses had been rubbed down, the men sat with a beer in hand. And they told the tale of the end of the pack and the fury of a stallion's retribution, with an old man sitting calmly on his back; a tale that over time would become almost legendary.

TWENTY-FIVE
Preparation

It was getting closer to the endurance ride and the stallion was so near to being ready; his fitness after the dog pack hunt had jumped up more than just a fraction; he seemed to have a clarity within him that was hard to explain.

The old man was as well as could be expected; he was dealing with a lot more cramp in his legs than before, and his breathing seemed to have become slightly more laboured. He passed this off as an adjustment to the colder weather, but he had long since given up kidding himself; it was becoming more and more obvious that his health was going backwards - and this time he felt that it was not going to improve.

When he had come back from the UK and left behind the crippling cold and damp, he had felt as if a great weight had been lifted. His stress levels had been reduced to practically nil, and an air of rekindled freedom had somehow coursed through his veins once again. There were also days when a feeling of great loss seemed to overtake him and he carried a sadness that he kept away from the world. It was on those days that his shoulders looked as if they were smaller and his body appeared to shrink. The tragedy stayed exactly where it lived, deep within like a one-act play waiting for the final curtain to come down. The story needed no audience and no witnesses.

The weather had turned its back on the clear, sunny hot days, followed by hot balmy nights and even though the clarity of the days was still there the cooler edge that it carried did not lead to warm nights under a single sheet. It was now cold and unfriendly and once the dancing flames of the fire dimmed to a small glow, the chill came into the house and entered the bones.

The horses had more rugs added at night to keep warm. Their winter coats were clipped so that after a hard ride the coat wouldn't overheat the body, or hold the water used after a ride. As soon as the water was poured over their steaming bodies a scraper was used to take the excess water away. If it stayed on the body it would defeat the cooling purpose by holding in the heat. This intensive strapping of the over-heated body was to bring down its temperature and slow down the heart rate that was often much faster than it should be. The quicker this slowing down was achieved, the more chance there was of the horse being sold to an Arab buyer, which in many cases was the sole objective of the competitive ride.

The sport of endurance had changed so much over the last fifty years or so. Enjoyed by purists as a means of pitting horse and rider against the challenges of Mother Nature, there was also a business side to the sport where money was a driving factor. The same was true with show jumping and dressage. Not so for the old man, he had a burning desire for one last ride out of the cold night and into the chilly morning and then hopefully into a warmer and friendlier day.

The days went by and the stallion's fitness was becoming more evident. When he was being groomed, he would affect the motion of fake biting. Turning his head towards the old man as the brush whisked its way over his body, he would bring his teeth together with a resounding click, his ears back and with the speed of the motion getting faster and faster. The old man smiled at these antics as he knew what they meant.

It was only when he sat on the veranda with his hands around his coffee cup that he would start asking himself the obvious questions: was he fit enough to complement the stallion's well-being? His bones seemed to hurt more than usual and his breathing was getting more and more laboured.

The diagnosis of bone marrow cancer on top of his steadily weakening lungs was something he had kept hidden from everyone since his return. His doctor and very old friend knew of course, and he would never deny the old man's desire for one last ride. They had known each other for forty years, give or take, and there was a mutual respect between them. Even though his body was maybe lacking slightly, his spirit was still unbelievably strong. His will to live had not been quenched; he was never daunted, just sometimes a little scared that one of his ailments might just overtake his desires. He would normally out-talk his fears, yet sometimes on very rare occasions a sort of common sense would cause a small amount of dread. And maybe if he dared admit it, a tiny fear that all was not as it should be. On this particular early evening try as he may, he was finding it hard to throw the feeling out of his head and disregard its annoying warnings.

The deeply embedded private thoughts of all the things that he had never done or managed to set straight in his life washed over him. The daughter he had not seen or even been in touch with, be it from logistics of location, or just that life moved on so quickly and before you realised, time had overtaken reality and not only a childhood had been lost, a whole life time had missed a beat never to be recaptured. So many losses and so much hurt, could it ever be made right? He was also remembering that he had never said goodbye to his father. They were on opposite sides of the world when he died. And he could not remember if he had told him that he loved him. They had a relationship that was a sort of mental competition. No one ever won. You always felt as if you lost. He felt a morbidity coming on and rose far too quickly, gasping. He reached for the coffee percolator and refilled his cup. Turning on the outside lights, he surveyed the farm and wondered how many more times he would do this before he…well, that thought was instantly thrown away. The lights went out and he returned to his chair and hopefully a whole new thought process.

He could hear the bookends as they purred loudly into the night, awoken as he scratched them both evenly and they responded with their usual zest. God help us, he would miss them so much. He then wondered if they would miss him - probably not - as cats were more involved with their territory than the people around them; strange really, as they could be so affectionate. Yet if you ever move house and take your cat with you - don't be surprised if one day it was not there anymore only to find months later that it had turned up at its old home.

Heading for the CD stack, he needed to change his mood back into a positive track. Pushing the relevant buttons the speakers came alive and the farmhouse was filled with the *Spencer Davis Trio* and *Keep on Running*. Down in the stables the stallion and the colt heard and felt the music and were uplifted by the sound. The old man was obviously feeling good within himself and shifting their feet they snoozed. If only they knew, then again better that they didn't; better if nobody did, for these feelings were private and carried more pain than most could cope with. There were times when he had trouble containing his thoughts but tonight his eyes closed, another day had run its course, and the long and forever sleep was getting closer.

He woke a little later than usual, with a stiffness that had crept into his body. Damn the weather - it seemed easier to say than to admit it was maybe to do with his age. The old man was getting tired, not just in his body, but in his mind; his usually positive approach to the world was becoming dimmer. It was Thursday and the endurance ride was this weekend; time to gather everything that was needed and start packing it all away in the truck. He had decided to take the small truck rather than the float. He sat for what seemed longer than usual looking around him with his coffee cup. What on earth was happening to him? His head didn't have the clarity he was used to and his bones felt like there was a fire inside them. He felt that there was something very wrong; he had suddenly become unbelievably tired, with nothing in his reserve tank.

He rose from his chair and went out onto the veranda, it was cold but he ignored it; for some reason it didn't matter if it was hot, cold - the nip in the air would normally have bought a comment like, 'Shit, that's a bit chilly,' but he just went down the veranda steps and started the long walk to the stables. He had never thought of it as a long walk before, it had never crossed his mind. The spring in his step was missing; the stable door and his beloved tack room seemed on another planet.

The two dogs, Squint and Pavarotti, seemed to be even closer to the old man than normal and were closely followed by the bookends, with tails going straight up then suddenly turning around like two question marks asking what was going on. This small parade arrived at the tack room door and as he opened it the two cats rushed in as if to surprise any mouse unawares. The old man didn't pay any attention to the bookends' antics, which was out of character.

He looked at the row of saddles and lifted one down from its place on the tack room wall. He then placed a spare pair of stirrup leathers and irons on top of the saddle; next, two spare girths and two bridles, bits, and a second Market Harborough or German Martingale; a running martingale, a spare crupper and six saddle blankets.

Then there were the day rugs and the night hoods - extra warmth just in case the weather turned bitter - which it could do at the drop of a hat. Sometimes there were rows of horses with their ears inside big, floppy covers, making them look like very large New Zealand meat rabbits. He always carried at least three extra of everything just in case it might be needed. You could never be over-prepared when it came to horses and

Mother Nature. Shin guards and rolls of bandages; his first aid box was the next item to be checked. Even though after each ride he went over all the gear, he never left the farm without double checking: liniments and home-made remedies for strains, sprains, swellings and anything else you could think of went into the emergency trunk. There were clippers and packets of safety pins, sticky tape and jars of coconut oil, other creams that did not heat up when leather or synthetic straps might need to be covered with something to prevent chafing.

Clean, unscented soap so if one of his horses looked as if it might be bound up internally, he would shave the soap into small slivers and dissolve it in warm water. And with a large syringe without the needle, suck the mixture up, administer into the horse's rectum then stand clear - as this would produce the same effect as a massive case of diarrhoea in a baby. But if caught on time, it worked and could avoid a very large vet's bill.

In fact you took with you anything and everything that could be used in the event of every mishap that could possibly happen, including shoes with cross bars and shoes without; safety boots and all his own apparel: extra trousers, jeans, jodhpurs just in case, shirts, socks, boots, different weights of jackets - not just for the weather conditions but to reduce and increase his riding weight.

Then there was the electric fence, extra batteries, hay and straw bales; a selection of feed to combat any change in the horse's appetite. If the home base was in a showground and the water had a strange taste because of the chlorine, he would add molasses. It was something he did at home even though his water came from a spring. As they drank it at home, it was safe to drink wherever they were. Too many times he had seen horses not drink at showgrounds and dehydrate before even going out on the track.

There were so many little tricks, most of them were plain logic; it was just that nobody seemed to think of them. Like, for instance, not taking hay from home and buying it on the way to the ride; the slightest difference in the horse's feed could mean the difference between winning, losing or not even making it through the vetting arena.

Tricks of the game, or common sense, one would like to think it was common sense. He remembered the day he watched one of the much older riders caressing his horse's cheekbone just under the eye and at the same time gently rubbing just below the high wither bone. One day, whilst sitting at the campfire he asked the rider, why? The reply was simple; look at your heart rate monitor or listen to your stethoscope and you will understand. The next time at the farm when taking heart rates he did just that and was amazed to see the horse's head slowly start to droop and his eyes close as if in a heavenly snooze, and low and behold the heart rate dropped down over three beats. This was enough to make the difference between passing the vet check or not; especially if it had been a rather quick entry to the home base on the final leg, against a rider who did not wish to hold hands signifying a draw. For some people, only an outright win would do at any cost, there are none so queer as folk, as was often said.

The old man had thought about maybe taking the colt along for experience; let him see what it was all about, the comings and goings of horses, and being held inside a hot wired yard. He would have the stallion next to him for company; it would be a great experience for him, even though deep down inside the old man knew that this would be his last ride.

For whatever reason, after this coming weekend, he knew would never ride in this race again. He felt a loss come over him even before the predicted outcome had even happened. And he walked over to the sprawling white roses that were just starting to show small buds in their sheltered position and he stood by the rails and leaned against the hard wood and he seemed to look right through the bush and the slab wall behind as if he had picked up his old friend the red dog from her resting place and was walking far away into the fields beyond. He stood likc this for possibly an hour or more.

The cold and a cramp in his leg made his eyes clear and he got himself together and walked back to the tack room. He lit a small combustion stove that sat in the middle of the room and pulled up an old chair from the corner where he normally hung his horse rugs and sat; it took a while to gather his thoughts and when he did he set about doing a recount of the things he would be taking to the ride. He let a small niggle come into his thoughts, 'Have you done this? Have you done that?' This was just a self-inflicted version of what people would say, building up how much they did by pulling you down, always looking for a failing, or a fault. Never just covering your butt and making sure you had everything necessary for a faultless journey.

He quickly moved along into another thought pattern and triple-checked everything again. It was for the horse's comfort, after all, and had to be right.

Satisfied that all was in order he started to mix up the night time feeds for the two horses in their stables. He had an old bath tub, elegant in a way, with its feet shaped like bull's heads. He would fill this with water and putting hay into hessian sacks he would immerse them in the liquid. This ensured that the horses had an added amount of water held in the hay sitting in their guts. Also he was one of the people who did not feed Lucerne hay for at least four days before a ride. Too often the richness of the undoubtedly beautiful hay meant that as the horse was trotting along the squirting from its backside took the much needed water content out of its body and laid it in a messy trail. What was needed was to see a neatly rounded ball shining as it sat where it had been deposited. Too often, precious water was lost by feeding over rich fodder.

…So much to learn and even more to be remembered in that small spongy area between one's ears. He grinned at his cartoon thoughts of a sponge desperately trying not to lose thoughts in the form of drips and the caption, 'waste not, want not'. It probably made no sense to others, but it gave him a chuckle.

The cats suddenly reappeared as the stove started to throw out a little heat and they sat there grooming each other enjoying the luxury of the warmth on what seemed to be heading for quite a cold moonlit night. The dogs had also come in and he closed the door so that the room could warm all of them up and take the tiredness out of his bones.

He always kept a bottle of whisky in the tack room for cool nights like this and he poured himself a medium sized glass and pulled the chair closer to the fire. He loved sitting here surrounded by the leather saddles and heavy horse harness and the smell of the leather and the dressing that he used on it had a very calming effect on him and his companions. It was good to be surrounded by what he felt was a form of security: familiar smells and his four legged friends.

It wasn't long before he had made up the two feeds and poured them into the two feed bins; both animals had put their noses into their bins and had started to give them their own special mix, moving the grains and the chaff around until it suited their eating habits. It was more of a ritual than a necessity and they loved to play with the meal before serious munching took place.

The old man had put three slight gaps at floor level and a small gap at the top of the tack room to allow some of the heat to permeate into the stables. He knew that it was an added entry point for the odd rat or mouse to invade from one space to another but with such avid hunters as the bookends he didn't think it would make too much difference.

With the insulation of the stables themselves and the warmth of the blanketed horses, the stables were quite warm compared with outside. He would load the truck in the morning and probably leave just before midday, which would mean he would arrive at the ride around 4.00pm. He would sleep in the truck, which was well insulated, with a cooker and a combustion heater. It was a lot warmer than a tent and needed less erecting time. All he had to do was to set up the yards, and banging in the stakes that held the electric wire was a warming job anyway.

He always carried enough horse water for the first two days and his well secured fridge and freezer kept his beers and meat cold, and enough ice for his strapping down of the horses after each leg of the ride. Bugger, the one thing he had not checked on was the electric heart rate monitor. He always took two and a stethoscope in case the monitors gave up the ghost. It had happened before, and it would again, no, it won't, he said to himself. This was his last ride, no need to worry anymore after this weekend. The sound of the horses eating and occasionally stamping their feet made him feel quite contented and he sat in his chair enjoying the heat. The simplicity of life was sometimes the most comforting and he felt his eyelids becoming heavy and his thoughts wandering off. It was not often that he allowed his subconscious to mull over things that were not pleasant. He had always managed to look on the positive side of things, whether awake or asleep. Tonight seemed different, his body tensed with a pain that came from deep inside, a recollection of things that he really did not want to dwell on; times of hardship, times of sadness. He awoke suddenly and he was sweating slightly, and it had nothing to do with the combustion heater. It was as if everything bad that had happened in his life had come to haunt him - as if he was going through a cleansing process. God, was this it, was it all over, was this a way of creating a clean slate to leave the only world he knew?

He really didn't know if he was ready to give up, there was so much more he felt he should do, so many things he hadn't seen, too many ventures he had not accomplished and too many people he had not said goodbye to. He got up from his chair and stoked up the heater and closed it down so that it just took off the chill. He'd be up early so with luck it would still be in or at least he could resurrect the glowing ashes and it would fire up very quickly. As he opened the door the cats rushed ahead of him and the dogs stretched and exited at a slightly slower pace.

The cold air had set in and his lungs tightened; winter had definitely arrived and he felt its cruelty grab hold of him and he nearly dropped to the ground. He put his arm out to stop himself from falling and as his hand touched the latch on the outside of the tack room door the coldness of the metal handle shot up his arm like an alarm going off inside him. He knew he either had to get to the house or go back to the tack room.

No, the latter wasn't an option, he had to get back to the security of his old comfy chair. The thing was not to panic, to just walk slowly, maybe even backwards so that the bitterly cold air was not going straight into his face. It sounded stupid, but it worked; slowly but surely, no panic, no stress, deep down inside he knew he would get there, and the closer he got the more he knew he must control his thoughts. It is that age old feeling of fear; the closer you got to where you were going, the stronger the feeling that you might not make it came to the fore. Control, old man, control, and know that soon you will be inside in the warmth and safety, with your dogs at your feet and a cup of coffee in your hand. Soon, you silly old fool, soon; don't give up and panic now. Think of the Aga and the warmth that was now so close. He started up the stairs and did not look up for fear of the distance looking too far. Look down one step at a time. The dogs stayed two steps behind as if out of respect or maybe they felt something more elemental at play.

Finally, he was there and his hand was on the door; it opened and the glow from inside enveloped him. The dogs were in and the bookends had made it too. He looked at the Aga and the coffee pot. He smiled and held the pot firmly and poured the warm liquid into his cup, his hands didn't shake and he stood there without moving for a minute or two. Then he made his way to his chair and sat down with a definite action. He called on every bit of inner strength that he had, and took in all the love and warmth that the room had to offer: the two dogs, the bookends, the stove, the fire, the hunting prints on the walls, the bridle that had been made for him years ago with every piece a moving item so that it would fit any size of head; the rabbit traps in the corner, all the things that over the years had come to him for whatever reason and held so much importance.

TWENTY-SIX
Endurance

He did not need an alarm call, he knew that if he woke up in time that was cool, and if he woke up late that was cool too. He would either arrive at the ride base early or late - or not at all - it really didn't matter, life would go on whatever happened.

The ride base was a hive of activity; people and horses everywhere, yards going up with white electric tape shimmering in the sun. Even though there was very little heat in its rays it was lovely to see and a lot better than pouring rain. One had to be thankful for small mercies. Camp fires of all descriptions were alight and coffee and steaks and sausages, anything that could be imagined on a barbeque, was cooking away on the grills.

Floats with canopies coming out from one side were set up with tables and chairs and people opening Eskys and drinking cold beers, wine and rum and coke. It was a typical ride base; some people working hard, others looking as if they might be thinking about it, those who just sat there giving orders and doing very little. It was just like ordinary life: those who did and those who didn't. Some of the horses and riders were going out to look at the course and some had already been and were waiting for the vetting arena to open. Trucks and floats were arriving in a steady stream. Some had travelled five or six hundred kilometres or more and some had only travelled a few miles. When all had safely set up there would be as many as one hundred and fifty competitors with as many strappers, if not more than there were riders. Some of the camps had three or four horses competing, some more, some less.

Most people knew each other well, and had their likes and dislikes among each other. Some, much to the criticism and disgust of others kept their horses lean and looking underfed. The reasoning behind this was usually concealed with the lines: 'they have to be tough.' It only ever made sense to those who said it. Sometimes they managed to get their horses through and then again sometimes they didn't. And there was always someone else to blame.

The showground was now filling very quickly; there were little floats pulled by tired four wheel drives and amazingly luxurious fifth wheelers and very large trucks with TV's inside and out; very small trucks with basic facilities, in fact there was every kind of horse transport imaginable. It was the most diverse collection of people who had one thing in common - they loved to be out there with their horses in all kinds of weather. Their reasons were varied, from the purist to the financially motivated. But the one thing that held them all together was to be one with nature and with their horses, the steady runners, the honest triers, and the flashy lookers all doing the one thing they loved, out there running hard and giving it their all.

It was a joy to see as they left the showgrounds with the first leg in front of them. That spectacle would be around 5.00 am the following morning. How this afternoon and night was spent was up to the individual, some partied hard, and some put in ear plugs and slept the sleep of the dead, waking only on their alarms to feed their horses during the night and check their water and shake their heads at those who had stayed up late enjoying the camaraderie of their respective camps, huddled round their fires, cans in their hands and stories and laughter on their lips.

As the old man drove his truck into the melee that the showground now was, people waved and called out to him,

"Hey, did you bring the grey, your little pocket rocket?" And, "Hey, it's really good to see you man, make sure you come over for a beer and a snag."

The greetings were many and all made with a smile. He was well known amongst the steadfast members of the various endurance clubs and had for quite a few years hosted his own endurance ride, well known for its famous parties, music and great sponsors. He believed that you did not have to win to get the big rewards, all you needed to do was complete and this was respected throughout the sport. They knew him for his laughter and his support for those less fortunate in their finances. Also his fairness within the sport; one or maybe two people said his own competition horses were unmanageable yet they were no trouble for juniors or the older members, only to those jealous of his popularity.

The pocket rocket that some of the riders referred to was a small grey, only fourteen two hands high; legally still only a pony, yet he rode like a sixteen hand horse, he was all muscle and guts. The old man had retired him about six years previously. He was a little gem of a horse with attitude like you had never seen before. He always rose to the occasion and was the most honest ride you could hope to sit on. He now wandered around a two hundred acre paddock collecting calves as his friends and rounding up the other cattle just for fun.

"Wait till I am set up and you will see who I brought, big surprise," he laughed to himself.

He had reserved his spot for two horses and paid his dues. At the last minute he had decided not to bring the younger horse; he wanted to concentrate on one thing - getting round the course safely and getting the stallion through vetting. To be thinking about a young horse in camp alone did not seem like the best idea in the world.

He lowered the ramp to the truck and was greeted by the two dogs wagging their tails furiously and grinning as only dogs can. They were both chained up in the rear of the truck and it was an adventure that Pavarotti had never experienced before, but old Squint knew only too well. He let them both off to relieve themselves and then chained them back up to the side of the truck till he had built the yard. He unloaded the stallion who blew himself up out of proportion just to let the other horses know he was there. He was not the only stallion competing and the others on the grounds answered his call as not so much of a challenge more of a 'we are here too' greeting. They knew each other from rides they had met on before. They were here not to fight but to keep their cool and compete. Some would control themselves and the newer ones could easily blow up and give their riders a very hard time. They all had to learn somehow and start somewhere so it was all good.

Being stallions, they had a more reinforced yard than the other horses, with more layers of electric fence, and in his stallion's case the wires were on taller stakes than the regulation height because the crafty old bugger had long since realised that if he was wearing a heavy night rug he could lean on the wires and possibly break them or dislodge them and not get bitten by the electric fence. So the old man added an extra wire top and bottom so that his fetlock or his nose, whichever came in contact with the wire first, would give him a big enough jolt to keep his respect of the flimsy yard.

The old man utilised the double space by making up two yards so that the horse could have a fresh area to stand in after the ride, before vetting, and it also made it easier to clean out after the night's rest.

He put a well soaked biscuit of rough meadow hay into the stallion's yard, having walked him round for about fifteen minutes just to take the stress of the journey out of his legs. He had stopped two times on the two hundred kilometre trip and taken the horse off the truck and walked him around a car park with grass verges to let him free himself up in every way imaginable. Now in his yard, the stallion had drunk deeply from his water bucket and was munching happily on his hay.

The old man now set about getting his sleeping area set up. Above the saddle racks at the front of the truck was a bed that pulled down from the roof of the truck and was held up by chains. It had a mattress that complemented his back, clean sheets and an electric blanket to ward off the cold. The site he had booked was powered and his truck was plugged into the mains. He had all his lights working and a spotlight trained on the stallion's yard; his TV and DVD player, music, microwave and heater - all the comforts of home.

He had Squint tied onto a swivel by the stallion's yard just to warn him if anything happened and to keep away any town dogs that might come around. And Pavarotti was chained up so that he could be in charge of the ramp and keep an eye on all the old man's personal possessions. It made the young dog feel very important and he took his responsibility very seriously, lifting his lip at anyone who came close to the camp and only coming off guard at the old man's say so.

With the stallion bedded down for the night and the dogs fed and chained, his next animal job would not be until about 10.00 o'clock when he would check the stallion's water and give him another hard feed and walk him around the showground for about half an hour.

So now was the time for a glass of wine, or a rum and coke, or maybe a gin and tonic… so many choices when you travelled within your own comfort zone. He opted for a pre-dinner G & T and fired up his gas cooker for a small steak and set about making a salad. Just then Pavarotti growled and there was a banging on the side of the truck. He looked up and there was one of his old endurance mates, a can of rum and coke in his hand and another in his pocket.

"Well, well, well, you old bugger, I knew you would be back," and throwing the can out of his pocket at the old man, he sat down on one of the collapsible chairs that had been tied to the side of the truck and said, "Get that into you and then come back to the camp, there's a mob there all waiting to say G'day and catch up on the news. Have you eaten yet?"

"Nope, I was just about to get it on now."

"Well old mate, don't, 'cause we've got heaps and you are most welcome, so come on down, lots of Rumbo and coke so let's get amongst it. You doing a 40 or an 80 tomorrow?"

"I was thinking of doing a 40," said the old man.

"Come on, do an 80 with us, you've brought the stallion, he will skip around or do you need to lie in, you poor old bugger?"

"That'll do, I've vetted in for 80; I only said I was thinking of doing 40, I didn't say that I was," he winked and they walked down the ramp.

"Guard, Pav," he said as he moved off with his friend, "Squint, stay," and they were off into the night, walking past other riders' camp fires and some camps that had already closed up for the night, all their gas lamps out and slight snoring coming from within their tents or floats. The steadfast players were of course partying around their camp fires, drinking, eating, and laughing, not really caring if they kept any of the other riders awake or not. There would be the usual whingeing and complaints made to the ride organisers in the morning as there always were. But this practice of sitting late into the evening had been part of the endurance scene for years and was not about to stop anytime soon.

There was a multitude of greetings from the camps that were up and actively enjoying the evening as they walked past and many invitations to come and have a drink. The two men stopped once or twice, only staying long enough to down a quick pre-mix before heading onwards to his mate's camp.

There was no missing it, all the die-hards were there and many in very fine spirits already. They would eventually beat the cold with alcoholic warmth and a Barrocca and a few aspirins to try to avoid the early morning fuzzy head that for some would be inevitable.

The morning chill and the burst of speed from the front runners would soon clear the cobwebs and most of the hard players were well aware of just how much they could party and still perform the next day. The die-hards would be completing the 80 kilometre ride in around the four hour mark, some even quicker, whereas the middle riders would do it in a respectable six and a bit and then there were the riders who would take advantage of the usual eight to nine hours allowed, which was a speed of 10 kilometres an hour. And as the motto was 'to complete is to win', this was a very safe and non-invasive ride time.

The front runners were there to register fast times in their horse's log books, mainly to entice the wealthy buyers to desire their mounts. You had to know your horse's capabilities to take some of the risks that these speedy riders took and be expertly knowledgeable about your strapping techniques. There were of course the inevitable vet outs - usually lameness or a metabolic problem. But 'them's the breaks', if you want to run hard, and a lot did.

The old man left the revellers at around 10.30 and headed back to camp to walk his stallion and fill up his water and give him his night time feed. Then he would retire to sleep if uninterrupted, till about 5.00am when the tannoy would give the wake-up call for the open riders, in fact he would probably be up before the call, as his sleep patterns were more deep sleep for short periods and then snoozes when his body or brain felt tired. His bed was warm and he wondered how he had managed all those years without the luxury of his electric blanket and of being able to plug into the mains if offered, or turn on his generator for lighting and heat.

The next thing he knew, he was waking to the sound of the stallion screaming loudly into the night. He left the comfort of his bed as the sound of hooves beating on the hard ground went past. Turning on the floodlight on the back of the truck, he saw with relief that the stallion was still in his yard, pacing up and down looking agitated at the sound of horses in a panic. Squint was up and growling and Pavarotti was standing on the ramp quivering with excitement at the noise.

It became evident that two horses had broken out of their yards and were rampaging about the showground at a rate of knots. This had woken most of the camps and there were riders and grooms rushing about all over the place trying to stop the free and now over-excited horses from causing any damage to themselves or any other horses on the grounds. There was whinnying and snorting of horses from all of the yards and the usual pandemonium that goes with loose animals.

The main objective was to contain the horses somehow and not let them escape onto the roads or break down any more electric fences. A loud shout of 'Got 'em!' came wafting across the grounds and as people were now up, fires were being re-stoked and more lights were being turned on. It was nearly 4.00 am so the old man threw the stallion one biscuit of well-soaked hay; around 4.30 am he would take him out and walk him about, letting him have a bit of a pick and acclimatise to his now floodlit surroundings. The sounds of water buckets being filled and general movement in the other camps continued and he realised how bloody cold it was. There was a near freezing breeze that had come seemingly from nowhere and was now making him shiver. Coffee, and more coffee, and change into his riding apparel best suited for such a cold morning.

He had put clothes that he thought he might need inside the bed covers so that they would have a semblance of warmth when he put them on. Once the ride started he would warm up with the speed of the start and the adrenalin rush, only his toes and fingers would remain cold.

He fed the dogs while waiting for the kettle to boil and then sat down in front of his heater to drink his coffee and warm up a bit. It was going to be an interesting day and he wanted to remember every bit of it. After walking the lad he took him back to his yard and gave him a small hard feed and another biscuit of hay. He could feel the horse getting more excited and he took off the top blanket leaving him with one heavy and one night rug.

Only an hour to go and the showgrounds had come alive. Most of the novice riders and the others who were doing the 40 km training ride had got up to start their day, even though they would not leave the showground until 8.00am. This was two hours after the open riders, who left in the dark, with their headlamps clamped tightly on their helmets and the horses' breathe leaving great clouds of dew-drop filled air on the rather cold, cruel, unwelcoming morning.

Having walked the dogs, fed and watered them, and groomed the stallion, the old man was mounted and out in the collecting area with all the other open riders, some walking round, others trotting and some cantering, all of them intent on warming up their horse's muscles and getting them set for the challenge ahead.

This was not one of the easier flat rides that appeared on the endurance calendar, where the riders who wanted to could clock up very fast times indeed. This one went high onto the mountain ridge which required the horses to do a considerable amount of very strenuous climbing. The old man recalled that as you climb up out of the mist and the low clouds you are suddenly blessed with the feeling that you are on top of the world with the sun kissing everything with gold, the tree tops below peeking up through the low lying clouds and the wedge tailed eagles soaring away above you. The world is a truly wondrous place and you are sharing it with a magnificent creature, ready to canter off along the flat track on top of the ridge.

For some of the riders, the picture was not the same as they had pushed their horses far too hard and the horses needed to stand, legs shaking, sweat pouring off them and not likely to pass the vet check on the first 40 km, let alone finish the ride. Hill climbs can be the most terrible traps for the slightly unaware rider and the downfall of many a young unconditioned mount. Yet for those who have worked hard at their fitness programme, what a buzz to be on top of the world and with a feeling of complete freedom - you could almost hear your heart singing with pure joy.

This was all ahead of the morning's riders as they waited for the clock to tick its way round to start time. Two minutes to go, two minutes, and don't forget to call out your number as you pass the start line, came the official's voice over the tannoy.

The riders started to get themselves into the positions that they wanted to be in at the off. The very fit and competitive crew would leave the showgrounds at a very fast pace, almost trotting out at 15 kilometres an hour at the very least, some trying to bring their horses back from an even faster canter as the fit horses were by this time pumped up and ready to explode into action. Then there were the just above steady paced riders, then the let's hang back a bit very sensible competitors and then the first 80 riders just out of novice and finally the riders who were there to complete who would normally wait until all the rest had left and just potter out at a very relaxed pace indeed. They would take all the time allotted for the ride and just enjoy the event, 10 km an hour was fine for them.

Then all of a sudden time was called and the front runners were off with a great burst of speed, their halogen head lights bobbing away as their horses left the showground for the first leg of the 40km.

The old man felt the stallion put in a half rear and leap forwards. He was used to being up front with the lead horses and was not going to be left behind. Within a hundred yards the old man knew there was something wrong, he could not breathe properly, in fact he could hardly breathe at all, he just could not breathe out against the push of air hitting his face.

He fought with the stallion, trying hard not to panic. It was hard trying to slow him down with the other horses around him going so quickly. He pushed his feet forward and lent back, not wanting to hurt the horse but desperately needing to slow him down. The stallion was so bunched up underneath him he felt like he was sitting on top of a volcano. He managed to turn the horse into the side of the track and put his head out of his line of sight of the horses in front. He fumbled for the grey inhaler and pushed the control button at least half a dozen times. He knew it would not work instantly and he would have to keep his old mate calm for at least five minutes before his lungs had a chance to recover.

Suddenly out of the darkness a voice said,

"Hey there, old mate, you OK?"

It was a rider from New Zealand who spent three months of competing time in Australia riding other people's horses and bringing them on for sale.

"You look like shit, come on, I'll walk with you so the old horse has a companion to keep him calm."

"Cool," said the old man and that was all he said for the next ten minutes or so, as he slowly got control of his lungs.

As his breathing settled he began to feel a bit more secure and he started to talk very slowly to his mate next to him,

"Shit, mate, I feel so bloody stupid, I just didn't realise that my breathing was so bad, I can't seem to push the air out of my lungs. This is crazy, maybe I should go back, it's just, well it was going to be my last ride."

"So what's the problem - I'll ride with you, this horse could do with a steady ride and if you feel bad at the 40 km mark just pull out as rider unwell. All cool, old man, all cool and groovy as you would say."

And they rode off together. When they came to a hill he just couldn't resist it, to hell with the pain, he just sucked on his inhaler and let the stallion go, and did they ever, they flew up and on reaching the top the stallion would stop and the old man would sit there and suck in air. After a while a silly grin appeared on his face and his mate looked at him and said,

"You silly old bugger, you are just having a ball, hey?"

And he nodded and as they set off on the flat plateau the very last riders passed them and the two men watched the young ladies' backsides disappear ahead of them, and now they both had silly grins on their faces. The rest of the 40 kilometres was a breeze, they galloped up the hills and down the step gradients. The stallion was so fit that to him it was a walk in the park - and the old man loved every bloody minute of it. As they neared the showground people were coming towards them and were saying, "Good luck with the vetting," as they thought they must be coming in off the 80 km in the last leg. So used to seeing them both doing 80's in the four hour mark, and they were coming in at around four and three-quarter hours. Little did they realise that the two of them were only just completing the first 40 km.

They called out their numbers as they crossed the line and the old man rode slowly to his camp, where he gently slid off his horse. His mate held the stallion as the old man slowly climbed up the ramp into his truck then got out his mobile and called his camp. In no time at all a couple of grooms had come over and taken both horses back to the New Zealander's camp, hosed them down and taken them through the vetting procedure. Both horses came in with very low heart rates and passing the check with no problems whatsoever. The New Zealander declared the old man as unwell to continue, so the horse had a clean bill of health in his log book and he declared himself as out of time to complete the second leg. The grooms looked after his horse and he took the stallion back to the old man's camp. He didn't wake his mate who was lying on his bed, he just covered him with a blanket and got back onto his own camp on the mobile.

People started to gather at the old man's camp and as darkness came they built a fire and drank and partied through the evening. He stayed at the old man's camp all night, wrapped up in a blanket by the fire with a few of the die-hards drinking on and telling old tales and stories that they had all heard before.

And the old man slept through it all. He woke with the dawn and felt as if he had been run over by a truck, his whole body screamed its objections to his every move. One of the girls called him down for breakfast and no one even mentioned that he had slept through the revelry of the night before.

After the awards had been handed out and people had helped packing up his gear and dismantling his yards, the New Zealander drove the old man's truck back to his farm with his two grooms following in his truck. They would all end up staying at the old boy's farm that night and make sure that he was OK, without him realising that there could have possibly been a problem. There were no comments made about his breathing, or his pain - which was so obvious - even though he tried hard to make it not be. Everyone was most respectful and he covered up his embarrassment with the occasional joke and a fair amount of yawning and a little snoozing quietly between drinks.

The day was done and it would be the last time he ever got on a horse again, only he didn't exactly know that at the time.

Deep down inside he knew that it was all over, he just hadn't let it come to the surface yet.

The next day found him alone and for the very first time he realised that to be alone was, for him the safest place to be. It had never really occurred to him before, being alone after all those years of having to be what others wanted to see him as. This was the only way in which he could actually be himself, and that was all of a sudden, very frightening. For no other reason than it meant he could relax, really relax, because he didn't have to prove anything to anyone, he didn't have to think, am I hurting someone? Should I be telling this story or this joke?

It was so ridiculous, to realise that he had lost so many years trying to please other people and not really pleasing anyone, for the simple reason that he didn't really know what any of them wanted. What they, in their lost way wanted was what he did not even know he had, which was his own personal freedom. If only he had seen the light, if only so many people like him had understood that what they had was their own self-worth.

It was that stupid thing called simplicity. He went out onto the veranda and after looking down at the yard below, he walked down the steps and past the stallion's day yard and looked long and hard at the white roses trailing up the slab wall. He thought to himself, 'those roses are so white, and my friend Fox is or was their initial food source.' The plants' roots had gone further down and were secure in their own depth; the red dog was no longer. He walked on to the stables and stroked the first head out of the box, which was the young colt. He put out his hand palm down, wrist up. Likening it to a nose coming forth looking to introduce itself. And the young colt extended his head and said 'hello', such was the understanding of their relationship. He then turned his hand sideways and caressed the horse's cheek and the young colt blew out and closed his eyes and laid the side of his head in the old man's upturned hand.

They were joined in their own way; they stayed like that for whatever time it was and then with a click of his tongue he broke the spell and rubbing the colt's nose moved on to the stallion's stable.

The old boy's head appeared immediately and himself was right there in all his magnificence, his head was arched, his nostrils flared and his mane hung like a mystical creature's wraith. The two of them stood there; two souls touching each other in a way that said hello and goodbye in one movement. It was as if they both knew that the time had come and they would never share the precious moments they knew so well again. It was all over and neither of them knew what that meant or what the over part was, but in their own way they were saying goodbye. Between them was a line to life that was breaking, not in a bad way - it was just coming to an end like a bluebell or a daffodil, or a day that becomes morning, and daytime and night.

The old man looked away, his eyes were moist probably because of the temperature change or maybe because of a pull of the heart.

TWENTY-SEVEN
New Beginnings

The auctioneer's hammer came down and people congratulated the winning bidders. At the farm, all was spick and span; there were no heads hanging over the stable doors, but there were a few chooks running about and a couple of peacocks. There were no dogs or ginger cats; Ollie the frogmouth owl was sitting in the barn but nobody knew.

There was no Otis Reading or Muddy Waters playing in the farmhouse, in fact there was no music at all. In the lean to there was a white rose bush in full bloom - defying anyone to cut it down - but apart from that there was nothing but a farm just sold.

There was a chair that sat alone in the kitchen, a chair that dared anyone to move it. There was a little girl in the yard going round and round in circles, every now and then she would change legs as if she was a pony having a lesson before going off to pony club.

Pony club, the grounding for many an international rider, or so they would all like to think; most of the boys would discover girls and most of the girls would discover boys and their all-important ponies would end up in a field eating grass and getting fat. Some, though, some of the young and terribly involved with their ponies would continue on to the next step, being a horse, and competitions and a way of life that was the joining of two spirits - wild and wonderful.

The little girl's parents were sitting on the veranda with the Real Estate Agent who had handled the sale and they were discussing the farm's history. As they talked the little girl came up the stairs and skipped on into the house as if it was something she had always done. The three on the veranda smiled at each other and the Estate Agent said,

"You know, I think your daughter is going to be very happy here."

"Yes, we think so too. The next step of course is to take her pony out of the livery stable and bring her down here, she is so excited about being able to see her last thing at night and then first thing in the morning, instead of having to leave her in someone else's care."

A slight chill had replaced the late afternoon sun and the new owners invited the agent in for a hot drink before he left. As they went inside the agent stopped in his tracks and said,

"Well, I'll be damned."

There, asleep in the old chair, was the little girl and two tightly curled up balls of ginger fur.

"I've been looking for them for weeks now, I always leave a bowl of milk out just in case they are around and it's always empty when I come back. You would never know if it was them or not.

"The old man who owned this place called them the bookends because where there was one, there was the other facing each other or back to back - hence the name. They both answer to it and have always been an integral part of the farm.

"I have his two dogs at his request, and I will take you up the mountain next week to see the two horses. They are the two mentioned in the bill of sale that live way up there in the top paddock. It's an old Arab stallion and his last son, who would be about eight years old now.

"They are the best of friends, the stallion stands with his head in a corner of the field and his back end facing outwards, as if he doesn't want to look out. He and the old man were great mates and I think he misses him in his own way. They're both friendly, the older one is a bit aloof and tends to stand alone most of the time. The bookends spent a lot of time with the horses and it wouldn't surprise me if that's where they've been.

"As I have the two dogs there was nobody here to talk to apart from Ollie of course."

The couple looked quizzically.

"That's Ollie the frogmouth owl, the old man had him since he fell out of a tree and he has had complete freedom of the house and the barns and the stables. Once he works you out, he will just appear and become part of the furniture.

"Your little girl will have a collection of instant friends. Just look at the bookends curled up in the chair with her now - the old boy used to say that if you had a chair that held you, then you would never need a dream catcher; all your hopes and dreams were right there in that chair. All you had to do was let go and close your eyes and the comfort of the chair would do the rest.

"One day, if you are interested, I'm quite happy to fill you in on his history - I think you might find it most fascinating; there was a lot more to him than most people knew about."

"We'd love that," said the couple looking down at their daughter and the bookends asleep together as if they had always known each other.

The agent put his empty mug on the draining board and wished them goodnight. And as he drove out of the yard, the lights in front of the house went out and the moon took over; the white roses shone, the bookends slept, Ollie fluffed himself up in the barn and high up on the mountain the horses slept as only horse's can. And the sound of *Billy Joel* mournfully singing *I wanna be your man*, came drifting out of the farmhouse settling into the timber of the stables.

And the old man's spirit lifted and wafted away to wherever spirits go when their time on this earth has finished and a new chapter in the farm's life had started and peace continued in the valley.

ACKOWLEDGEMENTS

A very special thank you to

Clive Farrell
Val George
Lance Kirkly – one of the best wildlife photographers in Australia
And Teddie Dahlin

…for their faith in my scribblings, because without them this book would still be in my head.

ABOUT THE AUTHOR

Photographer © Paul Harris

Although a lot of people remember me as Mike Abbott from the Bless this House with Sid James, my career started long before then–back in 1957 in fact!

I was in Regent's Park one day heading for a chat with the wolves at London Zoo, when a man called me over and gave me his card, which I duly put in my pocket and forgot about. My mother later found the card and I was thrashed for talking to strangers before she rang the number only to discover it was a Walt Disney talent scout.

I was sent along to a company called Progressive Management run by Neil Landour, who also represented Jane Asher, and we both became his child protégés. My first role was a cameo spot in the film Greyfriars Bobby, in which I played the part of Jodie Ross. The roles came in thick and fast – next was as series for the BBC called Deadline Midnight, in which I played a wandering Polack–ironic since I was a wandering Czechoslovakian of the same age–and from there I ended up at the Globe Theatre in London's West End, playing the juvenile lead as the son of Sir Ralph Richardson and Phyllis Calvert.

It was a jump into alien territory from there, literally! I was cast as the co-lead for the Saturday morning pictures on the episode called Masters of Venus (well before Star Trek). We used rocket ships made of Paper Mache crashing into paper rocks. How times have changed!

After the run at the Globe Theatre, my theatrical career continued when I was cast as Michael Gwynnand Diana Churchill's son, with Jane Asher playing my sister in the play Will you Walk a Little Faster. We did a pre-West End tour, arriving in London eight weeks later where Neil, my agent, showed up in his double-breasted jacket, twill trousers and bowler hat and took me to a theatre in London where the line of boys waiting for something, I had no idea what, stretched for three blocks.

Neil simply ignored the line and walked straight up to the stage door, spoke to the lady holding a file filled with the boys' names, and simply said to her, "we'll just go down to the stage". Having done no audition, and with no idea of what I was there for, Neil looked into the blackness of the auditorium presumably towards the producers and directors, and said to me, "When do you want Robin to leave for Canada?" Someone replied, "It'll have to be a week on Wednesday when he turns fourteen." I probably made a million enemies in one fell swoop.

The following Wednesday I was on my way by plane to Toronto to take part in the original cast of Camelot, playing opposite Richard Burton and Julie Andrews at the O'Keefe Centre in Toronto. Jenny Productions who presented Learner and Lowe's musicals had decided that Sir Tom of Warwick who closed the play with Richard Burton playing King Arthur, had to be an English boy.

So there I was, still only fourteen−Robin Stewart, a

Czechoslovakian immigrant, now British subject, becoming an American Alien – one of a small group of non-Americans to play Broadway. As well as Camelot, I was also cast as Ingrid Bergman's son in the series 24 Hours In A Woman's Life for CBS television, so I was working day and night.

After my stint in the U.S I returned to the UK to play midshipman in HMS Defiant, and I spent the next four years doing cameo roles in various police series.

Sadly, my mother died when I was only 16, and by the grand old age of 18, I'd decided that the acting life was just too much. I wanted to be an 'intrepid traveller' and so I jetted off to East Africa. I had the most amazing adventures in Kenya and Uganda, meeting many of the Great White Hunters of the time. When I got back to England a year later, I had no intention of acting again, but within a week I'd been offered a job, and so I took it.

Soon after I was offered the role of Mike Abbott – playing Sid James and Diana Copeland's son, in Bless This House.

I had a wonderful six years on the series, which also allowed me to do other work, including working with Sir Alec Guinness, when he played Charles 1 and I played his son, Charles II in Cromwell.

Tragically, Sid died of a heart attack on stage during one the Bless This House season breaks. With the TV series no longer in existence, I was suddenly offered an opportunity to go to New Zealand to compere their first telethon, which was for muscular dystrophy. After a bit of negotiation I moved to New Zealand to host the NZ version of Opportunity Knocks. Little did I know it would be only a few years before Australia would beckon in the unlikely form of an invitation from Derek Nimmo to go to the Melbourne Cup.

I headed off for Melbourne, and was immediately asked to be on various talk shows, including the Peter Couchman Show and the Mike Walsh Show. That all led to a role on Young

Doctors, and soon I was living permanently in Australia.

I had the good fortune to be offered the part of Macarthur in the ABC mini-series, The Timeless Land. But it wasn't long before I had itchy feet again, and while I was on holiday on Magnetic Island in Far North Queensland, I was asked to join the Townsville radio station, 4RR, where I started my own production company, which in turn led to a stint in Cairns as producer for FNQ. I also toured Australia as the lead in Up and Under, a show that had just won the Sir Laurence Olivier Award for best comedy in England.

During my years in Australia I had always made sure I had access to horses, and I owned several properties where I'd kept horses, but now I felt it was time to get back to the country, so I bought a rural property near Toowoomba and began to breed Arab horses for endurance. It was an even busier time than usual – I was producing a show called Midweek Live interviewing visiting actors and comedians, including people such as Ronnie Corbett. 1984/85 found me on the Sons & Daughters series for Channel 7 and providing many of the voices for Captain Kookaburra's Road to Discovery.

At the same time a chance came up to be involved in a new venture on the Gold Coast, so I moved closer to New South Wales, and a year later was asked to play Polonius in the Australian Theatre Company production of Hamlet.

At the end of this busy period I ended up on a property with my horses in Northern New South Wales, and for some time I concentrated on breeding, training and riding, as well as my writing. I created and promoted a local endurance ride – The Bonalbo Bash.

I now live in England and writing has become my passion. My first book is called Being Mike Abbott, about the time I was in the UK TV series and now this wondrous story about the old man and his animals. Writing gives me great pleasure and I hope to have more books out as soon as I can put pen to paper, or text to the ‘puter. It seems like a natural next step in my career…….

Lightning Source UK Ltd.
Milton Keynes UK
UKOW04f0016280515

252402UK00002B/116/P

9 781910 705131